I'M A JEW

I DON'T DO JESUS

MERLE D. HOGAN

Copyright © 2008 by Merle D. Hogan

I'm A Jew I Don't Do Jesus
by Merle D. Hogan

Printed in the United States of America

ISBN 978-1-60477-445-0

All rights reserved solely by the author. The author guarantees all contents are original and do not infringe upon the legal rights of any other person or work. No part of this book may be reproduced in any form without the permission of the author. The views expressed in this book are not necessarily those of the publisher.

Unless otherwise indicated, Bible quotations are taken from the NIV Topical Study Bible, New International Version. Copyright © 1989 by the Zondervan Corporation.

Some of the names in the book are of real people and were used by permission. All other names were changed in order to protect privacy.

www.xulonpress.com

Dedication

To Yeshua — Until the day I stand in Your presence and am surrounded by Your glory, I will continue to dance before You and praise You. Thank You, Lord, for loving me unconditionally.

To Paul, my husband and best friend — Thank you for letting me fly, and for being the wind beneath my wings. We've only just begun.

To Shana and Samantha, my canine children — I thank them for their continued patience while they waited for their water, meals, and walks.

I also dedicate this book to the memory of my dad, who passed away in 1998. He told me continually that I could do anything or become anyone I wanted to be if only I would just try. I thank him for telling me to let nothing stop me or get in my way, and for challenging me not to just dream, but instead to do what it takes to fulfill those dreams. He was always an encourager, even when I failed. Dad, I thank you for cheering me on.

I'm A Jew I Don't Do Jesus

To my dear friend Jimmie Walters of over thirty years, thank you for loving me without judgment and for helping me on one of the most important nights of my life. It was your patience, faith, and direction that led me to accepting Yeshua HaMashiach, Jesus the Messiah, for which I will be forever grateful.

Acknowledgements

Stacy Rhea, my daughter and my loving friend — You are positively an inspiration to me. With all my heart, I am so proud of the woman you have become. You truly are a gift from God.

Greg with a G, my son-in-law — When you married our daughter you weren't able to pick and choose us as your in-laws; we were part of the package! For that reason I thank you for your dedication, strength, and patience with our family.

Miss Stephanie Amanda, my eldest granddaughter — It was a blessing to be with you on one of the most important nights of your life. As we sat together in a small church in Georgia we were visiting, you gave your life to Yeshua. May you always remember that wonderful, special evening we spent together. Remember I love you Miss Amanda, far greater than the stars, moon and sun.

Shelby Rhea, my middle grandchild — I love your imagination and your ability to draw on paper what your eyes and heart feel. Please continue to draw. There is still a lot of room left on my walls. I find irresistible your gentle sweetness, hugs and kisses, and the way you still love to sit on my lap.

Daniel Gregory, my grandson who goes by the name Gregory — the amount of energy and talent you display in all sports is unbelievable. You have been one of the many joys in my life bringing much laughter with you wherever you go.

Victor and Dixie Oliver, Tom and Lucy Belt, and Partners In Ministry — Since 1990, many of you have been my mentors, friends, and family. Thank you for being with me in the best and in the worst of times. You have shown me the real true meaning and the understanding of the love Yeshua has for me.

Deenie McKeever, my mirror image — It has been a blessing and an honor that we have been able to practice and dance for many hours in worship to the Lord in many churches. My involvement in our Davidic Dance Ministry "Yashar" has been a special time in my life. May we continue to bless the Lord and others through our dancing for many years to come.

Barri Mallin – You're such a dear friend, and I appreciate so much that you have taught me to be positive in everything. You have always lived and followed the scriptures no matter what you have gone through. Thank you for continually reminding me that God has always been with us and forever will be.

Robert Solomon and Fred Goodwin Jr — Both of you have made a major impact in my life. I thank you for your teachings on what it means to be a believer in Yeshua, the true meaning of our holidays, and an understanding of the scriptures.

Jerry and Virginia Kasha, my roommates and great traveling companions — Thank you for your encouragement, your help in editing this book, and for our many long hours of prayer. Together we have shared many difficult situations, which has given us strength, wisdom, and a deep appreciation of the Word. You have sincerely enriched my life.

France Sinkwich — Going through our trials, we have been like two peas in a pod. Knowing God has been with us this entire time, we have been able to get through them. We will make it!

Contents

Foreword xii
1. It Was Just Home 15
2. God's Holy Temple 35
3. Sleeping Beauty 47
   God's Gift 54
4. But He's Not Jewish 55
   His Love 64
5. From Sickness to Sickness 65
   My Child ....
6. Once Again "He" Has Spared My Life 91
   Peace 99
7. I Want What She Has, But What Is It? 101
   I'll Come Again 106
8. The Night I Gave My Life to Yeshua 107
   My Husband, My Lover, My Friend 118
9. First to the Jew, Then to the Gentile 119
   Praise, Promise, and My Vow 127
10. The First Time I Thought I Could Help 129
    We Are One 138
11. Why Did I Do It Again? 139

	Father's Day 147
12.	There's No Such Thing As a Little White Lie 149
	Peace of Mind 157
13.	Every Second Counts 159
	Dad on His Deathbed 168
	Mom 169
	My Daughter, Stacy Rhea 170
14.	Mexico, Ready or Not, Here I Come 173
15.	Be Careful What You Pray For 187
16.	Witnessing God's Healing Powers 195
17.	Don't Judge a Book By Its Cover 203
18.	I Can Breathe 207
19.	God Still Moves Mountains 215
20.	Please, Just One More Time 227
21.	I Do 233

A Time for Everything 235

Glossary 237

Foreword

My story is written,
Not for glory or fame.
But to give honor to the Lord,
Father, Son, Spirit, all the same.

My childhood days,
I knew of His name.
When things went wrong,
The Jesus word I would blame.

From sickness and sorrow,
In tragedies and fear.
Feeling scared and afraid,
I just knew He was there.

Meeting my husband,
Families putting us to the test.
I knew, he was my true soul mate,
God only gives His very best.

The night Yeshua called me,
I was given a chance and a choice.
To accept Him, or forget Him,
My yes came out from within my voice.

He totally accepted me,
With an unconditional love,
My sins have been forgiven,
By my Lord watching from up above.

To get to know Him,
Is to rely and share trust.
I do love and adore Him,
His words and actions are just.

Relax and enjoy,
This story He has given to me.
Pass it on to others,
It's memorable, you'll see.

Chapter 1

It Was Just Home

I was born in Perth Amboy, a small city in New Jersey where everyone walked to school, most of us went to the same synagogue, we all had dark hair, dark brown or hazel eyes, and we couldn't talk without using our hands. My parents were in a circle of friends where every family had three children. We kids were all around the same age. Was it great planning among the women, or something in the river water?

Sound like a pretty picture, but do we sound boring? Not this small town. We were as normal as any other place: kids getting into trouble, clean trouble, family disagreements, families just being families.

I was born into a family of Jewish descent. My Hebrew name is Malcah (Queen) Devorah (Bee), and in English my name is Merle Debra. I am the middle child of three, with one sister three years older and a brother three years younger. Many say the middle one seems to get in trouble no matter what. The only funny thing about that is, as I started growing up, I was always in trouble simply because I was the troublemaker.

My mother has often told me I was such a quiet baby, always smiling, and I would sit in my carriage for hours just rocking myself back and forth. I was happy, comfortable and enjoyed being with myself just rocking.

Since those early days Mom has asked me quite a few times, "What happened to you?" ... "When did you start talking so much?" "Why do you talk to everyone?" "How can you have so much to talk about?" "Don't you ever get tired of listening to other people coming to you and telling you all their problems?" Even now when I need to relax, have a quiet time to myself and daydream, you will find me rocking in a rocking chair, alone with my thoughts for hours.

What I remember about Perth Amboy was the best childhood one could ever want. We lived there until I was 12 years old, but I can close my eyes and still see it as if it were yesterday. To some it may sound like a fairytale place, but to me, I just called it home.

My family lived in a two-family duplex. There was a large attic on the third floor and a very large room in the basement where my dad had an electric train set up on a large wooden table that he claimed was for all of us children. Behind the door you would hear bells, whistles, and smells of smoke that would come out of the engines. There were loud sounds of trains colliding when the track signals were not changed properly at the right times. The large table had villages, little plastic people, trees, waterfalls and two long sets of Lionel trains. Dad used the excuse 'the kids want to go down and play, the kids need more trains, the kids need, the kids want, the kids should have.' But whenever we needed Dad for something, we would find him downstairs by himself with the trains, but like he said, it was really built for all of us to enjoy.

Our family lived upstairs and a family with a son and a daughter lived downstairs. We were close in age. When I was ten the family downstairs moved and bought a larger home for themselves. My mom was excited because she wanted to move downstairs. My aunt and my favorite uncle lived for awhile in the attic on the third floor before they moved into their own apartment a few blocks down the street. Uncle always had a sweet smile. They were an older couple, thin, gray-headed and slow in movement. The only thing I remember about their place was it seemed dark and didn't have a lot of light shining through, and it had that distinctive smell, not of moth balls, but the smell older places always seem to have.

When we moved downstairs, my mom had white carpeting installed in the living room, sun room, and dining room. I could never understand, with the three of us kids running around, why she put in white carpeting. Mom wanted to redo the kitchen and found just what she loved, a fully-loaded pink kitchen. Everything, I mean everything, was pink, including the stove, refrigerator, and counters. It was like living in a blown-up bubble of bazooka bubblegum. Mom loved it and thought it was the newest and most beautiful color.

On one side of us was another duplex home. There was an older couple living downstairs. The man didn't like the kids playing outside and making noise. One day he stuck his head out the window, yelling at my friends and me. He said if we didn't stop making so much noise he was going to pour boiling hot water on us. It scared us at that moment, but then it became a joke to all of us. Many times we would tell the story of old Mr. Curley to scare our friends who came over to play. When we told them what he had said it would either quiet them or make them go home. Either way, I thought it was a great trick to use if ever I wanted to send someone home.

The space between our home and Mr. Curley's home was an alley about the width of a car. This alley was just barely wide enough for both families to get their cars into the back where the garages were located. Above Mr. Curley's home next door lived a friend close to my age. We would try and throw things back and forth through the windows. Occasionally, my ball would end up in Mr. Curley's home when his windows were opened. Many times his wife would smile, throw back our ball, and tell us to ignore her husband.

Next door to us on the other side was a very small alley between the two houses, only wide enough for one person to walk through. This small alley was where the water would drain from the backyard. Our house was so close to the one next door that we could even pass things hand to hand through the windows across this alley. Living upstairs in that house were two girls, one my age and the other my sister's age. When we lived upstairs we could look right into their house and even see their television when it was turned on in their sun room. We all got along pretty well for the most part.

Next door to the house with the small alleyway was a cute little ranch home where an older couple lived. Next to them was a two-set community tennis court. We used to play on the courts, but not with tennis rackets — just throwing the ball across the nets and then trying to jump over the nets, tearing up our clothes and breaking the nets in the process. My brother, myself and our friends would be sweaty, our clothes as dirty as could be, and we would sit outside the court with a smile on our faces and turn our heads away when others would come in and see the nets either on the ground or twisted and dirty.

The question we were always asked was whether or not we had any idea who made such a mess. Of course we would deny knowing anything.

Our entire backyard was cement. There were no flowers, dirt, or trees in any of the three backyards. One alley was shared with the garage path, while the other home had a green fence between the homes, which we climbed constantly just for fun. In the farthest area of our backyard were three one-car garages connected to each other. One of the garages was for our car, the next one held our outside toys and all our bicycles, the third one would have been for the other family living there before they moved out. When the weather was rainy and too bad to play outside we were allowed to play in the garage with all our toys. We were supposed to stay inside the garage, and sometimes we did. We would see Mom checking up on us by looking through the screened porch windows. We could see that smile of hers, then we would quickly run back inside the garage.

Mr. Curley and his tenants each had a two-car garage. Alongside of their garages was a large wooden bin that would hold two or three garbage cans. Each had a large wooden lid that made a great place to throw a ball and play catch. When it snowed, the snow would cover the entire tops of the garages and the garbage bins, and we were then able to slide down from the tops of them. Getting up to the garage roof was a chore, but the fun and laughs we had with our sleds was incredible. We hardly ever had to leave our backyard to have fun.

One time a friend of mine and I were playing bull. I was the bull and she had a make-believe cape. We were playing too close to the house, but I charged straight ahead anyway and accidentally rammed my head into a nail that was sticking out of the house. I yanked my head back and ran inside with blood dripping down my face from where the nail had made a large hole in my forehead. Mom cleaned it up and told me I'd be alright. She assured me that I'd had my tetanus shot and the hole will close up later. It did, but I still have a round scar in the middle of my hairline to prove how dumb I was to play the game of bull right next to the house. What did I learn from that experience? I learned I should have been the one with the make-believe cape!

Also in the backyard we had a green and white, double-glider swingset. We tried many times to swing it high enough to make it go over the top, but Mom always seemed to know where we were and what we tried to do before we did it. She was always at the back porch at the right time calling out, "What do you think you are doing?!"

Halfway to the garages there was a raised, broken patch of cement. It seemed every time I would ride my bike or run too fast I would fall down in that same spot. I always seemed to fall on the my left knee. It was always swollen, bleeding, and black and blue. One time when I fell down and really split my leg open, mom took me to the doctor's office. The doctor told me if I didn't stop falling so much on my knee he would have to cut it off. I know now that he was just kidding, trying to scare me straight, but when you are young you tend to believe the doctor and not your mom. I believe I became a little bit more scared, but I didn't stop falling or bleeding, nor did I stay away from that troublesome spot of dried-up cement. I believe after a while I might have been a little spiteful about it.

In front of our home there were short shrubs and some plants, but not many flowers. There were around five or six stairs that led to the front door and four cement stoops, two on each side of the cement stairs, where we would all sit while outside. We did not have any decks in the front, only our stoops.

Across the street from us were seven houses from one corner almost to the end of the block at the other corner. Next to the last house and facing them on the left was a large basketball court. In the summer we played ball, and in the winter the city would come in and fill it with water and make it into an ice skating rink. I spent most of my life on skates or in the water swimming. I skated after school each day and spent all my weekends on the skating rink until dark. My friends and I made snow castles and forts and had the best snowball fights ever.

Our house had floor radiators, and on each one of them would be my socks, gloves, hat, jacket, sweater, and shoes underneath. On the other radiator would be my brother's attire.

During school nights I had a curfew, but mom always had to send someone out to get me. We needed to do our homework, but I told Mom I was always finished even when it wasn't. My love was for the outdoors, and I would say anything to get Mom to let me stay outside just one more hour. Sometimes it worked, and sometimes it didn't, and when she figured out I was telling a story, I knew I better watch out. On weekends my brother and I never knew when to come in. We didn't want to spend time eating because that would mean less time to play outside. We would meet all our friends and have races and snowball fights, and we would wash each other's hair in the snow.

My dad believed we should be taught to swim at an early age, so he threw me into the ocean and pool waters, almost before I could walk. He told my

I'm A Jew I Don't Do Jesus

mom I would always come up, because it is natural for children to float up. She must have wanted to kill him, and once I became a mother I could understand completely, because he did the same thing to my child when she was very young, before she could ever walk, and it scared me so bad I screamed like bloody murder. I told him he was going to be the victim, and all he did was laugh.

As a family we would go to Asbury Park to walk on the boardwalk and swim in the ocean. At that time there were ropes from the shore extending out a long distance into the ocean where you could hold on to the ropes and walk if you were afraid to swim.

I remember when I was very young somehow my mother's hand let go of mine, a very large wave hit me, turned me around and took me under. I started eating sand and had no idea where I was, when all of a sudden there was a hand pulling my head up by my hair as I was choking and spitting out sand. I do not remember who that person was nor what happened afterwards. Even with that memory the ocean is still a wonderful, peaceful part of my life. I make sure every summer I go to a beach to regroup, walk, sit still in a chair in the ocean and just stare out and marvel at God's creation. I have always seen the ocean as a beautiful but dangerous body of water if not taken seriously, and I never turn my back on the waves.

Down a few blocks from our home the city had a large regulation baseball field packed with many bleachers. When there weren't any games being played by schools, my friends and I went to the fields to run. We ran the bases and ran up and down the bleachers, just having fun.

A few blocks' walking distance from my home was Penn's candy-and-soda shop where all the kids of all ages would hang out. We would buy our penny candy, Dots, Root beer sodas, bubble gum, and ice cream. Next door to the shop was where one of my sister's girlfriends lived. The older kids were always hanging around there, and us younger ones would hang around outside on the curb just to pester our sisters and brothers. The house had three cement stoops where the kids would sit. The only thing I didn't like was that all the older kids thought they could boss us around. We were within walking distance to everyone's home, and I found a few shortcuts through other people's yards to get to my home. The whole town was easy to get anywhere you needed to go by either walking, running, skipping, or biking.

About five long blocks from home was the YMHA – the Young Men's Hebrew Association. This was where the older kids would bring some of us younger kids after school (probably forced by their moms) to dance, snack, and just run around and have fun. We were supposed to be doing our homework, but the fun was much better. When I reached an age of learning to dance, my sister taught me how to do the lindy. We were the best partners and I had a great time. I remember one time my mom bought my sister and I matching grey poodle skirts and grey sweaters. I hated skirts; I had always hated skirts and I never wanted to wear them. Jeans and sweatshirts were

I'm A Jew I Don't Do Jesus

(and still are) my favorite attire. Those times at the Y were special times for my sister and me. We laughed, danced, and actually got along with no fighting.

Across the street from the tennis courts was the Raritin River where boats came to dock. Where the river met the ocean we were allowed to swim. In those days the water was pretty clear and clean. We were not supposed to go out too deep, so you can guess where I could usually be found! There was the waterfront with a boardwalk where we used to ride our bikes. We would put a card with a clothespin in both sides of the spokes on the front and back wheels of our bikes, and then ride on the boardwalk and make the neatest, loudest noises. On the boardwalk there was a very expensive restaurant called The Barge. I can't remember ever eating there, but halfway down the boardwalk was a stand where we could buy hamburgers and hotdogs.

Every July fourth the neighbors would get together and sit on the grass, bringing pillows, blankets, food, and drinks. When it became dark, fireworks were set off out from the middle of the river. All our friends and their families would come down to the river. I would always sit with my brother because he was afraid of the loud noises and would hide his head in his blanket. Of course, I made fun of him and laughed at him, but I also sat alongside of him inside the blanket so he wouldn't be afraid. I was the big, strong sister taking care of my brother. That was my job, and I enjoyed it sometimes.

From a young age I enjoyed playing baseball, soccer, basketball, and swimming. I remember only wanting to wear my hair in a ponytail. In the evening when I would take the band out of my hair there would still be a line around my hair from where the rubber band had been in all day. My sister was the one who played with dolls, doll houses, and bassinets; I was a tomboy straight from the heart and only wanted baseball bats and gloves, and to be outside climbing trees. No skirts, dresses, neat white socks and patent leather shoes for me; give me mud, dirt, sneakers — the messy look. I had many more boy friends than girl friends. The girls cared more about themselves than having fun. My dad always called me Messy Bessie, and I loved every minute of being a tomboy.

In our sun room we had a beautiful piano, couch, and television. Mom thought it would be great for my sister and I to learn to play piano. My sister enjoyed the lessons for awhile, but I disliked them from the start. I didn't want to practice or pay attention to my teacher. I wanted to go outside with my friends. After a short time my teacher told my mom she was wasting her money and her time, and it would be better if she discontinued my lessons.

My sister thought my brother and I were too weird for her. Our big sister was too grown up for us, and thought we were just mere children. In some ways I believe my sister was born mature. My brother and I were in a world of clowning around, and I was always in trouble. She was almost a teen, and it seemed as if we were too childish for her. My brother and I were great friends, and I took him along with me wherever my friends and I would go.

Always, I stayed in trouble with mom because I got him into trouble doing things she believed he would have never thought of getting into by himself. Since I was the older sister, it was always my fault. That was fine with me. We had so much fun doing the crazy things we did.

I remember as if it was this morning. I dressed in my new pink shorts outfit mom had just bought for me. I was told not to get dirty because she was having guests over. We were allowed to go out and play but were told to be back in an hour or so, and to please stay clean. My brother and I, along with another boy named Michael who was a friend of mine, went down to the river. We ended up falling in the mud in a drain sewer. We had an awful smell and you could not tell the color of our clothes. When we finally arrived home, the guests were already there. Mom met us at the back door, and she was not smiling. That sent Michael running home. I was told to strip off all my clothes on the back porch, take off my muddy shoes, leave them at the back porch, and go in and change immediately. Because our new carpet was white, we were always told to leave our shoes outside. Mom gritted her teeth and said she would deal with me later, and that meanwhile I was to get inside, change into some clean clothes, and then return quickly to the living room where I was to be on my best behavior. Mom put on her smile, turned away and went into the living room to be with her guests. I remember thinking *this will not be an easy night, I can tell already. Where is Dad when I need him?* Well, he was inside having a great time eating and drinking with the guests. My brother and I looked at each other and laughed, even though we knew we were in deep trouble. The only thing we could do was smile, be polite, and behave as best we could, and then maybe Mom would let this one slip by.

Mom had a way with us when we didn't behave. She would never hit us, she would just grab our upper arm, hold tight, grit her teeth and say, "Do you understand? Stop!" Most of the time Mom would call us aside so no one could see. I can still clearly remember one time when I didn't listen to Mom, and as she grabbed my arm I tried to get away. It didn't work. One of her long, fingernails went into my upper arm causing bleeding down my arm. The nail was imbedded in the skin. With difficulty we finally released the nail without it breaking off inside my flesh. I screamed, "Look what you did! Now my arm is bleeding and I have a hole in it!" She said if I had listened to her to begin with and hadn't tried to run when she grabbed me, nothing like this would have happened. I still have that scar on my arm, and all through my growing up years it served as a reminder that next time it would be better to listen to Mom when she told me to do something. Besides the arm-grabbing method, most of the time Mom would say, "Just wait 'til your dad gets home!" Nothing ever happened, though; he always let things slide by.

When I started fifth grade there was a new family who had just moved in one street down from ours. The son was my age. He had blond hair and blue eyes. That poor boy was fresh meat for the girls because he was so cute. I do not know what the other boys felt about him, but to every girl, he was the cat's meow. I was not at the age for dating, and he was not Jewish, so we were just good friends.

We had a blue bird that we called Pretty Bird. He always sang with my dad. Dad would clip his wings and let him fly around the house, or sit on his shoulder and watch TV with him. In our dining room we had a large tank of many different kinds of fish. I think Dad was the one who would feed them, but the tank was so large I do not recall who cleaned it out. We never had any dogs as pets. I'm not sure of the reason why, but Mom didn't care to have any other animals (and of course we only wanted a dog); she just told us no and we never asked again. I do not know if she was afraid of them or just didn't like the mess they would make. We also never had cats, which was a good thing, because I found out later that I am highly allergic to cats. Two of my friends had small dogs. They were cute, but I don't feel as a child I missed anything by not having dogs. After my sister, brother, and I grew up and got married, however, the first thing each of us did was to get pets. I have had dogs, birds, and gerbils. My sister has had cats and a dog. My brother, on the other hand, has had dogs, cats, goats, horses, cows, and ponies.

I attended Number Seven Elementary School, which was within walking distance of our home. Next door to the school lived the principal. He would sit on his deck until it was time for the bell to ring. He would smile, say good morning, and wish us a great day. That was when we were on time. If we were getting late, his face changed from happy to an expression that said *you better get going,* and sometimes to scare us into moving along quicker he would threaten to tell our mothers, asking, "Now what is your mother's name?" There was no time to stop so we ran for our lives. For lunch we all walked home to eat and then came back for the rest of the afternoon. After school he would be sitting on his porch again. I used to wonder if he really ever went into the school building or if he also cut school a lot.

The school had a Halloween costume day. We would all wear our costumes, and in the afternoon our moms would come and watch us walk around the block with our teachers and show off our costumes. I remember one year my mom bought me a hot dog costume. It had a hole for my head and the rest of the body had a hot dog with mustard, sauerkraut, and pickles on a bun. The length of the costume was from my head to my ankles. That was the only costume I can remember.

When a kid made it to the fifth grade and had a certain grade average in school, he or she could become a patrol leader. The duties included watching the hallways and making sure there were no fights, checking passes when walking the halls, taking notes from the teachers to the principal when needed, and making sure everyone came back to school after lunch.

I was excited to finally become a patrol leader. When the bell rang I would make sure everyone walked into the school. In the mornings we patrol leaders would meet in school for the first half hour while the other kids were in their homerooms. We would meet in a room where there were large cement blocks, and each of us stood on top of one. We were told what we had done right and what may have done wrong. We all said the Pledge of Allegiance and the Lord's Prayer. If ever our report card was not what was expected of patrol leaders, we would have to turn in our badge for the next quarter. We wore large metal badges with an arm band, and there was also a strap where we could wear it on our belts. I was off and on patrol duty many times in one year. It was very obvious if your grades weren't good enough to make patrol leader, because your cement block would be empty and the others would make comments as you walked by such as, "Guess you didn't study this quarter," or "You must've flunked some tests."

The boys were required to wear dark pants, a white shirt, and a tie, while the girls could only wear skirts and a nice blouse. The days we had an assembly we all had to wear white shirts. All in all, I loved attending Number Seven School. I have so many sweet memories from those years.

On the last day of school when I was in the fifth grade, I was sitting in the last seat of the last row nearest to the door. One of my boy friends was in the class across the hallway. He was sitting in the first seat of the first row by the open door of his classroom. He was rolling around a tennis ball on his desk. I waved to him and motioned for him to throw the ball to me. He shook his head no. I waved yes and mouthed that no one would see it. He threw it across the hallway to me and I threw it back to him. There was only one slight problem. When I turned around my teacher was standing in front of my desk. The bell rang and all were dismissed for their summer vacation except my friend, his teacher, my teacher, and me. They told us if it was not for the last day of school we would be staying after school and then detention would have followed. Then they dismissed us, and I couldn't help but notice how they smiled to each other and told us both to have a wonderful summer. They would not be having us in their classes next year, thank goodness. We ran for our lives out of school, then hugged and wished each other a great summer. Little did I know I would be moving next year, and would not be seeing all my old friends anymore.

One day I came home from school finding police cars parked out front and policemen in my home. My first thought was that they were there for me. No, I had not done anything so bad for the police to show up at the house, but I guess I was just so used to getting in trouble. It turned out that the cleaning woman Mom had hired stole some money out of her drawer and then stuffed it in the spigot of the bathtub. My mom just happened to notice where the money was hidden and called the police. The woman was escorted out, never to return.

One summer evening while dad was at work, we had just come back from swimming and were hot, tired and sunburned. We were told to take showers while mom started making dinner. Mom was cooking dinner on a broiler that sat on top of an iron shelf in the kitchen. When we were all dressed and coming into the kitchen, the steak that was on the broiler caught fire. Mom screamed for all of us to get out of the house while she stayed there with the fire and to somehow put it out. She took a chance by staying in there by herself. We three were her main concerns and she wanted us safe. I thank God she did not get burned and that the house didn't burn down. There was just some smoke on the walls and the smell in the house. As usual, Mom took care of everything by herself once again and cleaned the walls.

In those years Perth Amboy was a wonderful place to grow up. We felt secure, everyone fit in, and our front doors could be left open. I have not been back, but I've been told the town has changed tremendously. Our brick home is now covered with aluminum siding, the windows have been changed, and all our friends have moved out. Where there were flower beds, now there is cement. The boardwalk has been rebuilt and is beautiful, but the river is no longer safe for swimming. All the homes have been renovated to look more modern, and some of the stores were torn down and rebuilt.

A couple of times through the years I have driven past the exit for Perth Amboy, New Jersey, but I have never turned off the exit. Now that I'm an adult, I would rather not visit and see all the changes. I have so many sweet memories in my heart and mind. I wish for things to stay the way they were.

Chapter 2

God's Holy Temple

Shalom.
Hello and peace.

Sh'ma   Yis'ra'el adonai   elohaynoo adonai   ekhad
Hear   Israel   the Lord is our God, the Lord   alone.

Barookh   shem k'vod   malkhooto   l'olam va'ed
Blessed   (be) His glorious name whose kingdom (is) forever and ever.

V'ahavta   et   Adonai Elohekha b'khol l'vav'cha oovkhol nafsh'kha,
And you shall love the Lord   your God with all your heart and with all your soul

oovkhol   me'odekha.
and with all   your might.

V'hayoo   hadvareem   ha'ayleh, 'asher 'anokhee m'tsavkha   hayom
(And these) words   (these) which   I   command you   this day (shall be)

al l'vavekha, v'sheenantam   l'vanekha,   v'deebarta   bam
on your heart and you shall teach them to your children and speak of them

b'sheevt'kha b'vaytekha oovlekht'kha vaderek oovshakhb'kha
when you sit in your house, and when you walk by the way and when you lie down,

oovkoomekh, Ookashartam   le'ot al yadekha, v'hayoo
and when you rise up. You shall bind them as a sign on your hand and to be

l'totafot bayn aynekha.   Ookhtavtam   al m'zoozot
as frontlets between your eyes. And you shall write them on the doorposts

baytekha   oovish'arekha.
of your house and on your gates.

Hear O Israel, the Lord is our God, the Lord alone. Blessed be He whose glorious kingdom is eternal.

I believe one ought to be quiet when entering the Holy of Holies, giving the respect to the Lord that He truly deserves.

As I look back on my childhood, I know I didn't appreciate the beauty and the meaning of the synagogue we attended that was next door to the YMHA. When you are a young child sitting and looking out the window watching the snow falling, or thinking about the warm weather and how hot it is inside and how cool you could be swimming instead of sitting in the synagogue for hours, the beauty and meaning of the synagogue is the last thing on your mind.

In the writings of this chapter I hope to capture the wondrous excitement and the atmosphere of the temple where I worshiped God, and where my beliefs in the Lord started.

As you approached the temple courtyard, there was an eight-foot–high chain link fence and gates surrounding the grounds of the synagogue, which remained closed and locked when no one was attending services or cleaning inside the temple. Entering through the gate you would walk straight ahead to long, wide, deep steps, at least fifteen to twenty of them, which spanned the full width across the front of the synagogue. The front doors were of large, thick, dark wood. I realize I was young and small in size, but I remember the doors being large in width and height, and I always had trouble opening them myself. There was always a gentleman who stood outside to greet, help open the heavy door, and make sure we were quiet going into the foyer. There were four large doors across. The two middle doors were used to go into the temple, and when services were over the two outer doors were opened as well. The two side doors were a quick get-away for the kids as the adults always seemed to block the middle doors and spend too much time talking and hugging their friends.

Entering into the large, open foyer area there were two, sometimes three gentleman waiting to see if anyone needed assistance. Their most difficult job was to make sure all the kids were quiet before they entered the main sanctuary. These greeters would whisper hello, nod their head in acknowledgement, and see if any of the men needed a Bible or to borrow a *yarmulke* or *tallit*. The *tallit* is a prayer shawl worn by the men, and a *yarmulke* is a skullcap worn by the Jewish males in the synagogue and sometimes in the home. The young boys were only to wear a *yarmulke*. After they had their bar mitzvah at the age of thirteen, as a gift their parents or grandparents would buy the young men a *tallit* of their own, and the temple would give them their own Bible.

Off to the side in the foyer were the stairs leading up to where the women and girls would sit overlooking the entire sanctuary downstairs where the men and boys were gathered. The men and women never sat together.

To enter the inner sanctuary one had to go through two very large, dark, wooden doors. My dad always sat in his special place, which was the last seat at the end of an aisle next to a large wooden column reaching to the ceiling. He was able to lean against it during the long minutes of standing up in prayer. If he became slightly tired he could rest against it and not have his head bob back and forth if he felt himself drifting off to sleep at any given time.

The pews were of dark polished wood, and great for sliding around. The women sitting upstairs could observe every part of the service, such as men drifting off into a cat nap or the trouble the fathers might be having with the boys.

Occasionally the men would look up when the women's voices seemed to get too loud, and they would either look at us sternly and shake their heads, or point to us to be quiet. If the boys misbehaved they were sent up to their mothers and forced to sit with all the girls. During the holidays I remember especially the women's hats. Some wore tall hats with long flowing veils, while others just wore a piece of simple white lace that fit round the top of the head and was held on by a bobby pin. Only the married women wore hats or veils. The single women and girls wore nothing on their heads. The very orthodox women would never let their own hair be seen, and so they would wear a wig and/or a shawl to cover their entire head. I can remember occasionally taking short naps upstairs in a corner and mom would just let me sleep, I guess to keep me quiet. I had to wear dresses or skirts, white socks, and polished shoes. I was always very uncomfortable, and trying to keep clean was a chore for me.

Sabbath was from sundown Friday night until sundown Saturday evening. Before sundown Friday evening the Sabbath candles were lit. When the holidays began on a particular Friday night, Sabbath services lasted anywhere between three to five hours. There were extra prayers and added parts of the Bible read, and on the High Holy Days the service went all day Saturday without a lunch break. We were meant to be fasting for twenty-four hours. During the regular Sabbath weekends we would go home after the morning service and did not have to go back again. There were some who chose to go back to end the Sabbath in the synagogue. I was thankful Mom didn't make us go back.

The rabbi and the cantor stood on the raised portion of the altar. The table where the Torah was laid down flat to be read was of waist height, fairly wide, and made of dark wood. It was high enough to easily lay the Torah on it without dropping it. (It has been said that if a person drops the Torah for any reason the whole congregation has to fast for a month. I have never been involved in such a disaster.) The Rabbi would stand at the center of the table while the cantor would stand to his left. The cantor helps with the services and leads the chanting, meditations, and prayers.

We did not sing songs like churches sing; the singing is certain parts of the Hebrew service that are chanted in tune. The whole congregation sings, prays, and chants in unison and has time for deep meditation. The rabbi is the one who speaks and gives the sermon. The shofar, which is the ram's horn, or a trumpet, is sounded at the beginning of the New Year and a few other times during the year. The trumpet sound always brings wonderful chills to my body.

The rabbi, cantor, the elders, and the assistants in the temple always wore a large, white, long *tallit* while the rest of the men wore a short *tallit*. When the men prayed, chanted or meditated any time during the service they would pull a portion of the tallit from around their neck and over their heads to unite themselves with God in a one-to-one relationship. They would pray their hearts to the Lord for whatever was needed. There were stained glass windows around the sides of the temple. When the light would shine through onto the men chanting it was breathtaking. In unison the men sang in Hebrew. Their prayers that reached up to the balcony sounded like many angels surrounding the ceiling. Their voices of strength, joy, pain, and gentleness have left me with a precious memory I will never forget. I do so want to hear those voices when I am in heaven.

Sitting somewhat quietly in our seats for long periods of time has grounded me to respect the Lord's words and the men who read the Torah. I love listening to men singing in unison in an alto range. Attending worship services together and being involved together as a whole family is the heart of God. When one of the members of the family is missing, it is felt by the rest of the family.

I will always remember the mingled smells of the ladies' perfumes, seeing the stylish hats the women wore, the singing, the prayers that were lifted up to the Lord, the stained glass windows, but most of all the feelings I felt. It was as if I was in the Holy of holies with God's presence surrounding me. I had peace, warmth, and a sense of security.

Behind the rabbi was the ark where the Torahs were kept. The ark was made of beautiful wood and on the outside were the names of the 12 tribes inscribed in Hebrew. You would then open two large doors where the Torahs stood. The Torahs were wrapped in blue cloth with gold trimmings and a symbol representing some part of the Bible. It could be a Star of David, a symbol from one of the twelve tribes of Judah, or the Ten Commandments. The Torah was opened and read on the Sabbath, for the Bar Mitzvah's for the boys, Bat Mitzvahs for the girls, and on the holidays.

My Nana, who was my mother's mother, would come and visit with us sometimes for a few months at a time. Nana had been married to an orthodox rabbi. She read the Bible and practiced on a daily basis everything God's Words instructs us to do. Nana believed every word in the Bible and tried to live every day, just as God wishes us to do. We kept kosher in our home which meant we did not eat pork, bacon, or have any dairy mixed with meat as it instructs us in *Deuteronomy 14:21: "Do not cook a young goat in its mothers milk."* If we wanted dairy after our meal we would have to wait two hours. We used two different sets of dishes and two sets of silverware for everyday use, and for the Jewish holidays we would have another two sets of dishes and silverware. Nana ate only the things that were written in the first five books of Moses.

There was one thing I could never understand, and that was why we weren't ever permitted to eat pizza. Nana always said it wasn't kosher. It wasn't until after my grandmother became older, in her 90s, when we were told it was alright. To me pizza was kosher to eat because the ingredients were mostly sauce, cheese and bread, the only thing that made it not kosher was when meat was put on the pizza along with the cheese. I never mixed the two, so I have been eating pizza forever, not telling Nana. I can remember in the middle of temple services when we lived in New York, from temple I would run down a long hill, run one block over, order and eat pizza with my friends, and go back into services. Since all the men and the boys sat on the other side of the synagogue, Dad never knew where I had been. My mom, on the other hand, could detect the smell of the pizzeria on my clothes.

There are six days when you may work, but on the seventh day is a Sabbath of rest, a

*day of sacred assembly. You are not to do
any work; wherever you live, it is a Sabbath
to the Lord (Leviticus 23:3).*

From sundown on Friday evening when the Sabbath starts until Saturday evening we were not permitted to turn any of the lights on or off. Before we left for synagogue we would leave the lights on that we knew we would need once we returned home and for Saturday as well. For the full twenty-four hours of the Sabbath the television was to be turned off. The stove was left on very low because we were not allowed to cook; we could only warm up food. If I was the last one out I would purposely leave the television on low so that when we returned home it would be on for us to watch. Nana would remind us we couldn't turn it off. After a while my mom made sure I was never the last one out. The Sabbath was a day for us to read, sleep, and talk with one another. Nana would have loved for us not to go to the movies and run and play outside, but unless it was the High Holy Day, on Saturday afternoons we played as usual. The Sabbath should have been a day of complete rest, just as the Lord commanded us to do. During the High Holy days we were not allowed to ride in our cars. Walking in our best clothes and neat, polished shoes felt like the longest mile ever.

As I look back, I regret I didn't spend more time with my Nana. Running around with friends doing homework seemed more important to me than having to sit with her to get to know her better. Nana was the most warm, loving, and caring woman, and not once did she ever raise her voice. She read her Bible every day and prayed for everything. She prayed before meals, and again during and after meals.

If someone got hurt, had a problem, broke a nail, had a fight with a friend, whatever it was, my Nana had a prayer for them. I am sure, without a shadow of a doubt, that my Nana prayed for me continually, not only because I was always in trouble, but because of her love for all of us. I believe she wanted us all *to know God* more than what we *knew of Him*. Nana knew God in such a loving, positive way. She had true trust and a strong belief in Him. I never heard her use a curse word or ever speak wrong about another human being. Her smile could light up a room, and her silver hair was always neatly rolled up on top of her head. She was so dear. Her complexion was so beautiful, and the skin on her face and her arms was as soft as a baby's behind. As she aged she became more striking and had a peaceful look in her face. She was truly a child of God.

Holidays were always special, and Nana never had trouble cooking for large groups of guests. Her rule was she would cook and everyone else would clean up. She was a fabulous cook. There wasn't a thing she couldn't fix, from meats to desserts, and the number of guests was never a problem. It didn't matter if there were six or fifty-six, she cooked with a smile for all. Nana never used measuring cups or spoons, just a dab here and a small amount there. When my sister tried to get measurements and ingredients while Nana was cooking she would take whatever was in her hand and try to measure it. As we matured and cooked the meals, many times we ended up never measuring and just pouring, just like Nana had done.

One Rosh Hashanah holiday, after drinking four cups of wine I was very silly. The chore of taking care of dirty dishes belonged to my sister and me. On this particular night my sister washed while I was supposed to dry. As I dried the dishes from the rack I would put them on the counter, but this time they were too close to the edge. I started laughing at something and suddenly they fell to the floor and broke. My mother was not happy about this and told me I was never to dry dishes again. In my hilarity I said to everyone, "If I had known that would be the result of dropping the dishes, I would have done it years ago!" That comment was not funny to my mom!

I'm so grateful to have these memories, and that in my childhood I was given a beginning knowledge of who God is and who He wants me to be. A few years ago there was a fire in the old synagogue of my childhood and it burned to the ground. How sad it must have been for our Lord to see one of His temples go up in smoke.

I wish for those who read the rest of my story:
The Lord bless you and keep you, the Lord make His face to shine on you And be gracious to you: The Lord lift up His countenance on you and give you peace.
(Numbers 6:24-26)

Shalom ... peace.

Chapter 3

Sleeping Beauty

Where was I and what happened for three years of my life? I had this strange feeling of being like sleeping beauty; one day I fell asleep only to wake up and find that three years had passed by.

I can remember finishing fifth grade at Number Seven School in Perth Amboy, New Jersey, and entering the ninth grade at Nichols Junior High School in Mount Vernon, New York. I do not remember moving from one state to another. What happened for three years that I should have no memory of it? Who packed our furniture and moved us? Did we drive to New York? Did I ever say goodbye to my friends in New Jersey? At one moment I was a young foolish kid having fun in a childish way, then suddenly I was a young woman of teenage years. I grew up quickly in many different ways and was not sure how to deal with it.

I found myself with my family living in an apartment house in New York. I am thinking I am in the front courtyard taking a picture with my grandmother, the one who was my dad's mom. When did I get here? I have no idea when she came, or how long she stayed. I can remember asking myself, why are there so many families living in one building at one time? When we lived in New Jersey I never saw an apartment complex. We all lived in either duplex homes or ranches. I cannot tell you what our apartment looked like inside, who our neighbors were, or why we were not still in New Jersey. Looking back, it seems very strange for me to not know what happened to me in three years. I do not know how much time we spent in that apartment, and before I knew it, we were living in a different apartment house. This place was not far from the first apartment. How did we get into this building? Who moved us again? My goodness, where have I been again? When my family moved from New Jersey to New York, I started the sixth grade, and now suddenly I was in the ninth grade in junior high school. Why can't I remember the block of time from sixth grade through eighth grade? It is the strangest feeling to not be able to figure these things out.

I attended Nichols Junior High School for four years and it was not until prom day that that my memory had any affect on me or that I could tell what was happening. As I awoke from the missing link of my memory, I can tell you all the names of my teachers and the names of my friends. The assistant principal sat with me a few times in detention hall, a place where we became rather great friends. The last year in junior high I dated the senior class officer, sang in the choir, played field hockey, basketball, enjoyed art, went to parties, and had major fun. Was that the first year I played all those sports? and when did I learn to sing? All my friends were the same ones I had gone to school with the entire four years.

Of all the last days of school in the ninth grade, I can only remember the prom day. I went to the beauty parlor to have my hair fixed really special, but as soon as I'd left the beauty parlor I hated the style. When I returned home I washed, set, and combed my hair to the style I liked. It turned out better than before, and I was sorry my mom had wasted her money on the beauty parlor. I have no memory of the prom party itself, but I vaguely remember going to the party with a nice guy, and I wore a pink dress. On graduation day, I have no idea where the graduation ceremonies were held.

Attending high school brought better memories. The school had just been built and my class was the first class to go through their entire four years there. My friends were great, I received my driver's license, and I was dating a boy who was one grade ahead of me.

There were many evenings when I would tell my parents I was going to be at the library, when really I was planning to be picked up by my boyfriend to drive around the dark streets. During my last year of high school I was never in trouble in school or with my parents; my friends and I just had typical teenage silly fun. We would get together in large groups and drive to someone's home to dance. We were just friends having a great time.

The day President Kennedy was shot I was busy smoking in the girls' room after cutting my history class. The bell rang, and as I came out of the bathroom hoping I didn't smell like smoke, I noticed everyone was crying and screaming as they gathered in the hallway. When I asked what was wrong, I was looked at as if I had two heads; then I learned what had happened, and not long after that school was dismissed early.

Graduation day was on the football field of my high school. The sun was shining so brightly, and it was very hot. We were all wearing white graduation robes and a white, four-cornered cap. I had only eaten breakfast that day because the excitement was more than I could handle. My parents were in the bleachers smiling and so happy that I'd made it to graduation day. After graduation our family went to visit my grandmother, my dad's mom. The entire family was taken out to dinner to a very expensive restaurant for my special occasion.

It was at this dinner I learned how to drink my favorite alcoholic drink, a Brandy Alexander. The drink was sweet and tasted like a malted milkshake. Since it was my special day, I was allowed to drink as many as I wanted. By the time I had finished my third drink, the room started spinning and I felt really nauseated. We were served our meal, and after eating I felt a little better, but oh my, the headache I started to get.

I had gone to my boyfriend's high school graduation during my junior year of high school, since he was one year ahead of me. I can distinctly remember the dress I wore, which was baby blue, the same color as his jacket. My hair was teased high with a flip on the ends. But oddly enough, when it comes to specific memories of my own graduation, I have no recollection of going to my graduation party. Did I go to a party? If so, who was there? Did I spend time with my friends? It is hard to believe I can't remember my teen years in New York when memories of the first part of my life in New Jersey are so vivid. It's not that I blanked out the memories from being unhappy, because I enjoyed my friends, especially my close circle of best friends; most of us stayed best friends all through high school.

So, what is the problem with my memory during those years?

There was one major sadness I will never forget no matter how many years I live. One of my very best friends in high school was having a very difficult, sad time at home with her parents. Her mother was sick and wheelchair bound. Her father worked, but her older brother never wanted to help. She was responsible for feeding, washing, and giving medicines to her mother. She lived in an apartment house across the small street where we lived, in the same complex but facing our bedrooms. I lived on the first floor while she lived on the third. We could wave and signal to each other. When there was trouble we would lower the shades. My girlfriend was never allowed to date so we would lie and tell her parents she was with me. She was never allowed to be herself, have fun, be with all her other friends at parties, movies, or just be wild. Things became so difficult for her and an overwhelming sadness seemed to come over her. She didn't laugh anymore and was always hanging her head low. Then one night we spoke silly stuff to each other on the phone, waved to each other through the window, and I went to sleep. Little did I know that my best friend had downed most of her mother's medicine, went to sleep wearing a new sweatshirt her brother had just bought her, and never woke up. I could not go to her funeral, I knew why but I wished there was something else I could have helped her with, and now my best friend was gone, gone from my life forever. At this time I had never had anyone close to me die. It was the most difficult and painful time of my life. To this day I can still see her smile and hear her crazy stories. I missed her very much.

After graduation I met two girls who were sharing an apartment together. I spent a great deal of time with them. They had many booze parties into all hours in the morning, and they introduced me to some of their so-called friends. With this group of friends there were drug parties, while others did a lot of gambling. Down the street from their apartment was a cute little neighborhood bar we would frequently go to, at least three times a week. My actions and priorities started to drift down the wrong path, a direction I did not need to go. I knew it would all be downhill from there if I didn't rescue myself from this crowd. I was able to disconnect myself from these girls, but not from the habits I had acquired.

Many times I have brought out my junior and high school yearbooks, looking at the faces of my friends and teachers and trying to recall those years. Some memories are there from the fun and happy times. I just can't believe most of school was a blur. Looking back on it now, I realize it doesn't really matter, because my adult years would hold the best times of my life.

God's Gift

God has given me a dear precious man,
To honor, to love, and to trust.
To follow his footsteps with kindness and grace,
Through hard grounds and in uprooting dust.

My life would have been so empty,
For he showers me with protection and strength.
Surely goodness and mercy shall follow him,
The Lord's favor will be of great length.

When he touches me I feel his passion,
His voice of gentleness and grace.
His eyes shine as blue sparkling sapphires,
Love and compassion smile deep upon his face.

Lord, humble me to you and my husband,
Let me empty myself and confess.
I need help from you both in righteousness,
For I know, you are gracious to bless.

I thank you, Lord, for my life and for Paul,
For his love, and gentle compassion.
I promise to be his companion through life,
With great wisdom, and a witness, to all.

Merle Debra
1998

Chapter 4

But He's Not Jewish

If you were to ask my daughter what religion she is, her reply would be, "I'm an Irish Roman Catholic Jew."

Growing up I was raised as much an orthodox Jew as my husband was raised an orthodox Catholic. Paul was the sixth child out of eight. His parents made sure the family attended church regularly, dressed properly, and tried to act civilized, especially in church. They went to church every Wednesday afternoon for religious instructions as well as on Sunday mornings, and they were all baptized and confirmed. Paul went to a public school from kindergarten through eighth grade and finished the last four years in a Catholic high school.

When I met Paul in the summer of 1967, he was working as a lifeguard at the beach club to which my family belonged. His hair was light brown, bleached from the sand and sun; he had a beautiful suntanned body and was very well built. I had blond hair (what was called "bottle blonde") and wore small bikinis. We both had that lust in our eyes and wildness in our hearts for each other. We were both dating others but that didn't stop us from wanting to date. We started our relationship by getting in a car accident on our first date. After coming out of a restaurant-bar, having only had two drinks, Paul sweetly helped me into the front seat of his car. He walked around to his side, smiled with that devilish smile of his that could always make me melt, and started the car. Instead of putting the gear into drive, he slipped it into reverse and gunned the engine. Looking through the back window, behind the car on a cement walkway was a shiny metal pole standing about waist high which kept the cars from hitting the curb. As we went full force into it, my head went back and forth very hard and fast. Whiplash! Paul stepped out of the car to check the damage. There in the middle of his metal bumper was a smooth, large, concave dent from top to bottom. Oh well, I guess that is what happens when you try to impress a girl and act debonair on your first date! Was I impressed? Not one bit! But did I think it was funny? You bet I did! From that day forward I christened Paul's car "Clarabelle" after the clown on the Howdy Dowdy Show. The car never worked the way a car should. The small metal locks on the car would always fall out, the heater never blew warm air, only cold, the steering wheel never turned a full circle, and the wipers didn't clear the rain or snow from the windshield.

The next morning when my family showed up at the club without me, Paul asked my father where I was. Dad told him they had to take me to the emergency room because of the whiplash I'd suffered, and he told Paul that if he ever went near me again he would kill him (figure of speech, of course, but my dad was pretty angry about it). Paul called me many times but my parents wouldn't let me speak with him. He even tried calling me on my sister's phone, but she would tell my parents. We started seeing each other behind my parents' back. At the beginning I believe it was mostly out of spite and lust for one another. We know now, however, that God had plans for us to be together no matter what we thought the reasons were then.

After a while my parents knew I was sneaking out and that Paul and I were spending most of our time together. Our relationship was growing more serious no matter what they tried to do. My parents eventually decided they might as well give him a chance. At this point in time it was all they could do.

One Friday evening at the request of my parents, I invited Paul for our Friday Sabbath dinner. My mother was not too excited about the prospect but decided she would give it a try. Mind you we were a kosher home. We were having kosher meat, chicken, potatoes, and vegetables. Mom asked Paul what he would like to drink with his meal, and he replied he would like MILK. My mother smiled politely and called me into the kitchen, where she laid into me: "What is wrong with you? Why did you bring him here for dinner? You need to get him out of here as soon as possible." Before I could even begin to answer she went on, saying, "You have always dated a Jewish boy, but now when you start to get serious with a guy, why does he have to be a Gentile?! I want him out! He needs to leave!"

I returned to the dinner table, calmly gave Paul some water to have with his meal, we ate very quickly, and then I told him he had to leave. He had no idea until I walked him to the car what I had endured in the kitchen with my mother. Inviting him to dinner was a mistake, a huge mistake.

After dating for a year we talked about getting married. Neither one of our parents wanted this. His mother wanted him to marry a good little Catholic girl whom he had been dating at the time I met him. My mother wanted me to marry the good Jewish boy I had been dating, who was in college studying to be a doctor. All Jewish mothers want their daughters to marry a Jewish doctor or a lawyer, not a Gentile anything.

The day I told my mom we wanted to get married I was told I had to ask permission from my grandmother, my Orthodox Jewish Nana. Mom told me with a smile on her face that if Nana told me no, then her word would stand and it would be final. I believe my mom thought Nana would say no and thus my mom would be off the hook from having to make the decision and be the bad guy. I think Mom had it all figured out: Paul would have to go and a nice Jewish boy would come into the picture.

It didn't turn out that way.

Nana and I went into my mom's bedroom alone. The bed was high off the floor sitting on a beautiful dark wooden frame. Nana sat to my left side. I respected her and would have done anything she wanted of me, but I was afraid this would all go wrong.

I told Nana, "Paul and I want to get married."

She looked into my eyes and asked me, "Do you love him?'

I told her, "Yes, Nana, I do very much."

She then said, "Then you shall marry him." When mom heard what she said I thought she was going to strangle my grandmother. It wasn't what my mother expected to happen nor was it what she wanted.

One night as we were going out on a date, before we were to meet a few of our friends we stopped in front of my apartment building. Paul looked at me with his beautiful smile that has always melted me, took out a small box and opened it, then asked me if I would marry him. I cried and said yes. My small diamond engagement ring is the most beautiful and priceless ring I've ever owned, then and now. As I cried with happiness he put the ring on my finger. I could not wait to show it to the world. My friends were the only ones who knew of our engagement, so when I was home I had to hide it in my pocketbook. We were really serious now; there was no turning back. When I mentioned marriage to my parents, Mom told me I was not permitted to get married before my older sister. (It is not our custom to give the younger daughter in marriage before the older one, as taught in Genesis 29:26.)

Finally, my sister became engaged and was married in March of 1969. Paul and I were then allowed to set our wedding date after the Jewish holidays. We were afraid our parents would change their minds, not only about the date we chose, but about our getting married in general. We needed another plan. We were going to get married no matter what our parents told us. I decided to ask my sister and her husband to stand up for us at a civil wedding.

Paul was in the army at this time, and in order for him to come home for the weekend I first needed to make an appointment with the Justice of the Peace. The arrangements were made and we were put on the schedule. When our scheduled day came the four of us went to the home of the judge. Paul and I were a little nervous, not knowing what to expect. The judge answered the door and escorted us to an office he used in his home. We were asked who the other couple was and I explained they were my sister and her husband. When we went downstairs he asked me my maiden name. The next thing he said scared me to death.

"I know your dad very well."

Then he looked at both of us and asked me, "Do you *have* to get married?" (meaning, was I pregnant), and I shook my head several times and said "No!"

He said, "Then I will marry you."

With a red face and an awkward smile I asked him if he was going to tell my dad. He waited a few seconds, looked at all four of us and told me no, but said it would be a good idea if I told him. I nodded my head yes, but knew I couldn't, not now anyway.

The service was short but to the point. We paid the fee, then shook hands and left. Now we were two married couples. The hard part was to keep this a secret, and my sister and her husband had to swear they would never tell. They never told and neither did we.

Now that we were married Paul's monthly pay allotment check for the month went from $40.00 to $80.00. The only problem was that I had to continue living at home to keep up the ruse while he lived on the army base. He would come to see me as much as possible but had to go back to his parents' home to sleep. Still, no one knew we were married.

The months were ticking by. My sister had been married in March. Paul and I had our civil service in April, and now it was May. My mom told me if we wanted to get married within the next month or two, it was too soon after my sister's wedding and so we would have to pay for it ourselves. I was working by then and Paul had little or no money, but we decided to get married in June. I drew up the guest list and made all the plans and the food. It was decided we would have a small wedding in my parents' apartment with a few friends and family members present, and a conservative rabbi would conduct the ceremony. We knew that because we were of two different religions an orthodox rabbi would never marry us. I did not want to be married by a Catholic priest, because that would be too much for my parents to endure.

On the day of the wedding we were not sure if Paul's parents would attend. When Paul left in the morning from his parents' home, his father told him he still had not made up his mind. Finally, both his parents and a few of his family members came. Some of the other family members were against this wedding and felt it should not take place. They chose not to come. It's pretty comical — after we were married, two of Paul's sisters married Jewish men!

Paul looked so handsome in his army uniform with his neat, short hair, very trim and fit. I wore a white, very short mini dress, and my hair was almost down to my waist. Our apartment was packed with friends and family from both sides. It was a beautiful sunny day outside and nothing was going to rain on our second special day.

I did not understand what the rosary beads symbolized, nor had I ever seen anyone pray with them. During the wedding ceremony I turned around, for what reason I don't know, but sitting there in the middle of our guests was Paul's mother praying with her black rosary beads. I looked at Paul with a puzzled look. He had no clue what was going on. As we were finishing the service, the last thing was to have Paul step on a glass wrapped in a napkin to symbolize our love and healthy life together, according to Jewish tradition. He raised his foot, brought it down, and smashed the glass into many pieces.

We stood facing the front windows in the living room. Off to the side in the dining room against the wall was a wonderful selection of meats, vegetables, fruit, and a fine looking wedding cake.

I had a few seconds to pull Paul aside to ask him what his mother was doing. I had to know — was she praying for my death or what? I couldn't understand why she was praying with blacks beads, especially at our wedding. He tried to explain but I still didn't understand, and I just had to let it go and enjoy our special day.

One of my uncles and his wife were present at the wedding. She was a Gentile. He could see on the faces of both sets of our parents that they were truly not happy about our getting married. I was so grateful for what happened next. He and his wife rounded up both sets of our parents and explained how his wife was a Gentile. He explained how there is nothing wrong with it as long as the husband and wife love each other. Then he brought over some Challah for all of the parents, said a prayer, broke the bread, gave each one a piece of it, and told them to get over it. My father and Paul's mother were given a drink, and my mom and Paul's dad smiled and shook hands. Finally it was a happy day! Thank you, Lord, for small favors and wonderful uncles.

Paul's parents still do not know about our first wedding. My parents, on the other hand, were told, but not until thirteen years ago. Something came up during a discussion with our daughter and my parents and it just slipped out. Oh well!

In 2007 we celebrated thirty-eight years of marriage. Way to go, God! I'm glad He knew what He was doing.

His Love

I bring you peace, love, and joy,
You gave me sorrow, pain, and hate.
We need to pray and ask for forgiveness,
Before for some it's too late.

I love you, My children, always,
Sometimes it's hard to see.
Call out My name, and seek My wisdom,
At the end, it's only you and Me.

God has one purpose in our lives,
To have us follow Him.
His paths are straight, with righteousness,
He forgives us of all our sins.

My love is always with you,
Through trials, tribulations, and pain.
Just call My name, loud and clear,
My Spirit will rekindle your flame.

Merle Debra

Chapter 5

From Sickness to Sickness

I can still remember the questions that swirled through my mind during the years of being an army wife and thus continually on the move: *Where do we belong? Where is our home? When do we get to stay in one place longer than a year so we can settle in?*

Between the years of 1969 to the present, we moved from:

Rockaway Beach, Queens, New York, to …
Fort Hamilton, Queens, New York, to …
Rockville, Maryland, to …
Aberdeen, Maryland, to …
Cincinnati, Ohio, to …
Wilmington, Delaware, to …
Fort Huachuca, Arizona, to …
Raintree Apartments, Roswell, Georgia, to …
Liberty Square, Roswell, Georgia, to …

Our present home, which is still in Roswell, Georgia.

Paul was in the army from the years of 1968 until 1976. During those years we moved so many times. I was a committed army wife, which means you go where they send you or you live alone.

Our first home was in Rockaway Beach; we had a small apartment downstairs in a fairly nice home. We had one bedroom, a living room, tiny dining area, and a small kitchen. The home was considered off-base housing quarters, which meant we had to pay extra for the enjoyment of living there. The owners of the home lived upstairs and were an older couple who were glad to have us rent from them. We were quiet, clean, and we both had jobs to pay for the rent. The most exciting part about this home was the fact that it was one block from the ocean. Getting to work was another story.

I worked on the east side of New York City. There was a bus stop right outside our door, so I would take the bus to the subway stop in Flatbush, Queens. The bus driver and I became good friends. He would wait outside my door, and if I was running late he would blow the horn and wait a few minutes more for me. The first subway ride took me to Grand Central Station on 42nd Street. From there I changed to another subway and went from 42nd Street to the east side of 46th Street. Upon reaching 46th Street I walked six blocks to 52nd Street where the office was located. Every morning while on my walk, I always stopped at a favorite little coffee shop where I would grab a cup of coffee and a large roll with an excessive amount of melted butter dripping from it. The office closed between five and six every night, and on a good day it took me two and a half hours each way to get to and from work. Whenever it snowed, or on the cold winter nights, it sometimes ended up taking an hour or so longer. In the winters I left in the early dark hours of the morning and came home in the pitch black darkness of night.

One early morning I remember coming up out of the subway in New York City, when all of a sudden, plop, plop, a pigeon decided to leave large amounts of poop on my head. I ran to the nearest bathroom in the closest building, which was a school. I tried to wash my hair with soap. The smell was still there no matter what I tried. Finally I got into work.

As I walked past my boss he asked, "What is that awful odor?"

I told him it was my hair. When I tried to explain to him what happened he just kept complaining about the smell. He sent me to the bathroom again to try to clean it out. The other two girls in the office couldn't stop laughing. I used every possible type of smelly soap he had in the office. I offered to go home for the day and try to get the smell out. Of course he then replied that the smell wasn't really so bad after all. He knew how many hours of traveling time it would take me to go home. It wouldn't pay for me to come back to work, so that was not an option. Both of my bosses smoked pipes, and that day they kept their pipes burning all day. I don't know which smelled worse, their pipes or my pigeon-poop hair.

Paul and I had been married only one month when our first disaster came into our lives. On this particular day the sky was clear, but the day before it had rained and there were puddles of rain and very slick grounds everywhere. I was working in the city while Paul was working on an army base not far from our home. I received a phone call from one of the men at the base. His story was that he believed Paul was working on his car antenna when he had a small accident and was now being sent to the hospital to have it checked out. He had no more information. I told my boss what happened and that I would like to go the hospital. He suggested I wait for another phone call to find out more details. Sound advice, I thought.

Shortly after that phone call we received another call. This call was different. I was told Paul was working on something and his hand was blown off. With that news I passed out. After being revived my boss and I wanted more information of the true accident. A few seconds later another call came; it was from the ambulance driver. While Paul was at work he had an accident and his ring finger was partially ripped off. The skin was torn off and half the bone was broken off. I had to make a quick decision of what to tell the doctors to do with his hand. I had two options: one was to just take the rest of the bone off down to the knuckle, and the other was to take the rest of the finger off and move his pinky over to be near the rest of his fingers.

My boss was on the other end listening. We told them to just take the rest of the bone off and leave his other fingers where they were. With that I passed out again. It is one of the hardest decision one has to make when you can't see the hand and you have to make a snap judgment. What if it is the wrong one? How do you know what the patient would want? Your decision is made for the other person, and whatever that decision is, they have to live with the final results. I sure hoped it was the right one for Paul. I didn't know what he would want. My choice would be what I felt was the best thing for him. Thank goodness for both of us, it was the right choice and Paul and the doctor were pleased with the results of his surgery.

After being revived again I called my sister who lived about an hour from the city. I told her what had happened and asked that she come to get me and drive me to the hospital. The ride was the longest and worst trip of my life. To get to the hospital we had to take a ferry. Small ferries always made me sick. My sister stayed with the car on the bottom deck while I had my head hanging over the side. The weather by this time was wet, nasty, and chilly. Paul was in a ward and I finally got to see him. He was very doped up from the medicine, and his hand was wrapped up with blood all over the bandages and on all his other fingers. He had to go to the bathroom but would not use the little urine bowls they gave him. He stood up with his gown open in the back, grabbed his IV pole, swayed from side to side for a bit, and yelled to everyone in the room, "I have to go to the bathroom, the real bathroom, not the small things they expect you to pee in." My sister and I and all the other men in the ward had a good laugh. When Paul came back from the bathroom he was able to tell me what had really happened.

Paul had been working on a radar antenna forty feet up. He slipped as he started to walk and his wedding ring got caught on the spoke of a fence, ripping his finger off, but it saved him from falling all the way to the ground, which possibly would have killed him.

We made it though the ordeal, but I struggled with why such a thing had happened to us already. *What does all this mean? We've only been married one month. Does this mean our parents were right and we were not supposed to get married, or is this the beginning of bad marriage happenings?* I was nervous whenever I would think about it.

In 1970 our daughter Stacy was born in an army hospital in Queens for $1.75. It was a wonderful time in my life. A beautiful new child, a home at the beach, not having to work for awhile ... I was in heaven. Only it wasn't long before the word came down from army officials that it was time for us to move. We received army base housing so we wouldn't have to pay extra money for our living as we had done to have our cute little home near the beach. We had enjoyed living in that little house, but with another mouth to feed we had to live in base housing.

We moved to Fort Hamilton Army housing in New York to an apartment house that felt all closed up. From the very beginning this apartment was a disaster. It had patched-up work all over the walls, it was half-painted grey, and it was peeling from ceiling to floor. We lived on the fourth floor, and there was no one around for me to talk to.

Being alone a lot was not good for me. I began to eat and drink differently. I started going through a six-pack of soda every day and did not eat properly. My stomach felt as if it was being eaten alive everyday with pains, and I started losing a lot of weight. I had tests run, but I was told I was only nervous from being alone most of the time and being an army wife. I was given Valium and stomach medicine. Nothing seemed to help. I gradually took more and more medicine, which brought me no relief. I felt worse with every day that passed.

Most of the time in the winter it was difficult going outside, so my daughter and I would dress in our winter coats and open the window in her room where we would sit and rock on my rocker. At least that gave us a change of air. One late weekend evening, out of the blue, the electricity in our refrigerator turned off. We had just been to the PX to do our shopping for the month and now everything had a good chance of spoiling. Our infant daughter's milk, all our meat, and everything else we needed to make our meals was in the refrigerator. We had spent our monthly allowance with nothing left over to buy extra food if all the food spoiled. I called Paul, who was working on the army base not too far from home. I told him what happened. He went to his commanding officer, but no help was offered at that time.

I was not one of those wives who said, *oh well, we will make it through this somehow.* No, I had to do something drastic. I called the commanding officer of the entire army base. It was dinner time, and after three rings a gentleman answered the phone. As kindly as I could, I said, "I'm sorry, I usually do not make calls during dinner time on a weekend, but our refrigerator just burned up. We have been to the PX and have bought our food for the month, we have an infant, and there is a chance all her food will spoil. What will you be able to do, and how long will it be before someone comes out to check it?"

There was a stunned silence for a moment, and then the officer replied, "I'm sorry for your inconvenience, ma'am, but I'll make sure you receive a brand new refrigerator within a few hours."

I thanked him and hung up the phone feeling jubilant that I had won this small battle!

Paul came home in time to receive our new refrigerator. Shortly afterwards he went back to work, and as soon as he arrived his commanding officer called Paul into his office. He was instructed that the next time his wife had a problem, she was not to call the commanding officer of the base. That was not protocol for this problem or any other situations. In other words, 'keep a handle on your wife and keep her mouth quiet.' As Paul walked out of the office all the other men smiled and jokes went around the base for a few days. Off the record, though, Paul's CO thought it was a cool thing that his wife had enough guts to call the commander of the entire base. I became somewhat of a better army wife after that incident!

Paul's first overseas orders were given for him to go to Korea, and together we decided it was not a place for our daughter and myself to go. My parents were living in Rockville at the time, and they invited Stacy and I (and our dog Princess) to live with them until Paul returned home in twenty-four months. Stacy was only six months old when Paul left, and she was two years old when he returned.

I had been to a few doctors within that time about my stomach problems, only to find no answers once again. I went to many doctors and had every test in the world inside out and upside down. I was sent to Walter Reed Hospital and Bethesda Hospital. If it was good enough for the presidents it should have been good enough for me. Not so; no one could find anything wrong with me, and now I was down to eighty-five pounds, still unable to eat anything. Then another problem started. I was experiencing the worst dizziness, which led me to stay in bed more often. The doctors still had no idea what was wrong with me. I was given more tests, stronger valium, more pain medicine, stronger stomach medicine, which all made me very tired. I was not able to care for our daughter. Some days I couldn't even function.

Paul finally returned home and then it was off to Aberdeen Proving Grounds in Maryland. We had a cute little two bedroom duplex home there. We were happy and enjoyed life there together. Our neighbors were wonderful, their children were great, and their dogs were well behaved. We went bowling every Tuesday night, and on every Friday night we played cards together. Along with three other families we took turns in each other's homes sharing dinner and snacks and having a great evening together.

Whenever Paul and I wanted to go out for an evening we had a great fourteen-year-old girl who babysat for us regularly.

When our daughter was about the age of two, she was riding her tricycle with one of the older girls standing behind her helping her push faster. Stacy's ankle twisted and became stuck in the spokes of the wheel, which broke her ankle. I was still having dizzy spells and a weird ringing in my ears, and I still had stomach problems and was taking too much medicine. It was difficult taking care of her. She wore a full cast from her ankle to her thigh, and even though she had been completely potty-trained, she had to go back into diapers until the cast came off. It was all I could do to take care of myself, let alone my active toddler. If I was staying downstairs for the day Paul would bring Stacy and all her toys down so I didn't have to go up for any reason. If I didn't take extra medicine, I had trouble functioning and life would pass me by and I would not realize what was happening.

We spent thirteen months there and then the orders came again. Paul was to be shipped off to Okinawa, Japan. Now what were we to do with not enough money to live on? I called Mom and Dad again. Dad had been transferred and they were now living in Ohio. We put our furniture in storage, kept out our essentials, and once again Stacy and I moved in with my parents.

While in Ohio I found out I was pregnant with our second child. I had mixed emotions about this news. With Paul always gone, I didn't want to go through this by myself. At six months things turned for the worse. I had been using an off-base doctor because the army doctors were too far away. I went into the office one morning and told him I had been feeling pains, like labor pains. After examining me he told me I was in the beginning of labor. I was given a shot to try and stop the contractions. I didn't want to lose our baby. I was tired and wanted to take a short nap.

Mom and Stacy went to the playground to get some fresh air, play for awhile, and let me rest. It wasn't long after they left when the pains really started ripping through my body. I started bleeding heavily and passing huge clots. I became scared and worried, and I needed my mom to be home with me. When they arrived home I was in the bathroom crying and in so much pain. Mom called one of her friends, who took care of Stacy while Mom drove me to the hospital. By that time I was losing too much blood and feeling very weak. After being checked into the hospital, the pains became worse and I lost a lot of blood. Quickly I was put to bed until the doctor came. All of a sudden I felt no pains; just like that they were gone. I called to the nurse and told her my pains had stopped. She started yelling at me saying I must have aborted the baby and that now she would have to go check the garbage can and go through all the blood to see where it was. At that point, I passed out.

I remember waking up flat on my back, with a white light staring in my eyes. It was not heaven, it was the operating room. Standing above me was the doctor and his assistants in masks. Their voices panicked and they screamed, "Oh my God, she is awake!" With that, I passed out again. I have no idea how long I was in the operating room, but while there I was given four pints of blood. The doctors never told me this. I found out a few months later when the hospital billed me for the blood. I tried to get word to Paul about what had happened by calling the Red Cross. Paul had been moving around a lot to Saigon, Viet Nam, and other places. Five days later when I arrived home he was finally contacted. I was told by the Red Cross that I did not have the correct zip code to try and find him. By then it was too late for him to try and come home. The day I was to be released from the hospital my parents told me we were moving again. This time our family was moving to Wilmington, Delaware. We loaded up in one car and drove, with me lying in pain across the back seat of their station wagon. I began having worse dizzy spells and stomach pains, and now my chest was starting to feel funny. By now I was having trouble digesting food. What was this that was happening to me? I was taken to many doctors, had many tests, which never show anything. More valium, extra strong stomach medicine, and now added pills to help with pain. We kept hearing the same story over and over again. The tests showed nothing. I was told that I was nervous because my husband was out of the country, and that there was nothing wrong with me.

I finally found a doctor who took pity on me, I think. He performed a test that inserted a tube down my throat to see if there was a blockage. Alongside of him was an assistant in training. I was given a strong dosage of valium in an IV and something else for pain. The IV went into the veins and took effect faster than pills. It seemed to have more of a calming affect on me since I had to swallow the tube. As it was going down the doctor was looking in his tube with a small camera attached to it, and suddenly he became so happy. Poking his assistant he exclaimed, "Look, it was an inflamed hiatal hernia!" They kept pumping air into my chest to be able to see better, and at this point I had had enough and pointed to get that tube out of my throat. My throat was sore for a couple of days but this didn't bother me; I had finally found out why my chest hurt so badly. I was then put on different pain medicine and a diet to help with food, only to find out my stomach never felt better. The dizzy spells now kept me in bed all the time. I will always be grateful to Mom and Dad, who were wonderful to me during this time, taking me to so many doctors at all hours of the day and night, driving me to have tests taken. At this point I was really ready for Paul to come home.

After being gone for a little over a year, Paul returned home. His orders this time were for Arizona, but it still felt too far for me and my parents to be separated. They had helped Stacy and me through so many things, sat in so many doctors' offices only to hear, 'there's nothing wrong with her' time and time again. They believed in me and never told me I was nuts or crazy. I received the best care one could ever ask for from her parents. I became so close to them I couldn't believe we were moving to Arizona, which felt like the other side of the world.

Moving day was an extremely hard day for all of us. My heart ached so badly. Paul and I, Stacy, and Princess started out on our long road trip across the country. On the way I got the flu on top of all my other ailments. We had to stop in a hotel an extra day for me to recover. Throughout all these things Paul never complained or became short with me. There were no army bases for us to go to, so we kept driving slowly. It took us twelve days to go cross country.

Until the army could find us housing, they put us up in a hotel where we basically had one room. The elevation was so high and I was smoking two packs of cigarettes a day; thus, my oxygen level was not as it should have been. All I was able to do was eat and sleep. Stacy would have to play most of the time in our dark, small room. Because it was taking the army so long, they moved us into the smallest trailer in a trailer park. Our daughter's bedroom was so small she couldn't sleep in her room because of the nightmares she had every night. That left three of us sleeping in a full size bed. There was no place during the day to go without a car, and no place nearby to walk to. There was nothing to do. Finally base housing became available.

We were in Arizona a total of three months and I was speaking on the phone with my parents every day, sometime more than once a day. I missed them so badly. I became so lonely, especially since Paul's work sometimes took him hours away, and most times he had to stay away for a day or two.

My parents came out to stay with us. What a great time we had, with only one major problem: our car broke down. We could not go for any long rides. I was feeling a little better and would have more good days than bad ones. We could drive to the places that were close, like shopping. There were no beaches, but we did have a large pool the army personnel and their families could use. It was better than sitting at home doing nothing. The weather in Arizona was mostly comfortable. Even though the temperature would reach one hundred and twenty degrees there was no humidity.

After my parents left to return home, I started with the sharp stomach pains again. I was taken to the base doctor. I was told he would have to do an internal examination. Of course this was nothing new to me. After examining me he told me he believed I was pregnant again and would have to do a "special test." He said he would have to put a long metal instrument up into my body. This scared me to no end. If I had any red blood that meant there was something wrong and he would have to abort the child. I was taken into the examination room with his nurse. He inserted the metal rod into me, and I wanted to die, the pain was so bad; it was worse than anything I had ever experienced in my life. As the doctor rolled me out of the room I remembered my husband and child were sitting in chairs waiting. The doctor said to Paul, "She is pregnant and I have to kill the baby." I was rolled quickly into the operating room, given IVs, and in no time the procedure was completed. I came out as angry as could be.

I tried to write to the army to tell them of what the doctor had said, the notes he wrote, and how displeased I was with the army. The only thing I learned from that experience was that you can't fight the army. A letter was sent to me to try and smooth the waters. I was so angry with the army, and God, and everyone around me.

I was plagued with tormenting questions that I directed at God: *Why, God, did you not let me have my children? Why did they not form properly enough to be born? Why are other women having two or three children and I have only one?* I didn't find the answer but I realized how special our one daughter is. I know I am blessed with having at least one child born who was born healthy. For years I was angry seeing other women with all their children, and friends would carelessly say oh, you only have one child. They didn't understand the ramifications of their comments, but it hurt me so bad I would cry and hide in my room. Paul and I know how special our only child is to us.

At this point dizzy spells were keeping me in bed most of the time. I had double vision. I couldn't drive because I couldn't make out where the middle line was since I was always seeing two. I couldn't read books or magazines because all the words were doubled and I didn't know where the words began and where they left off. I had high-pitched ringing noises in both ears, and pains in my head had started to afflict me. Doctors would never listen. Tests were always negative. Why was I like this? Some days were much harder than others. My daughter had to do many things by herself. We were living on an army base and hardly anyone could speak English. Living next door to us was a family from Viet Nam, and their daughter used the outdoors as a bathroom. They would bury *kimshi* outside in holes. Across the street a woman found her husband sleeping with another friend's wife, and she came back to the house with a shotgun shooting several rounds trying to kill him. I couldn't take it any longer. Living so far from family and being alone all the time, I just wanted to get out of the army and go home, wherever that was meant to be.

Paul received orders to go to Korea again. I wanted out of the army. I told him it was either the army or me, because I could not take it anymore and I was leaving. We had moved constantly for nine and a half years. I was sick, getting no help and not getting any better, and now he had orders to leave us again. I couldn't handle that anymore. He agreed to get out of the army and get his discharge papers drawn up.

A company in Georgia offered Paul a job. I can still remember a little chant that went through my jubilant mind as we cut ourselves free from the army: *We are out, we are history, we are gone, give us the discharge papers, you will never see us again!* We drove straight through this time from Arizona to Georgia. This time it took us only four days, traveling twenty-four hours non-stop.

Once we had completed the move to Georgia I was as sick as ever. I had spent more than ten years being bedridden, not able to do things for myself, and I was getting out of control. One evening we decided to go out for dinner and I ate some fried chicken. I can't tell you how sick I became. I had excruciating sharp pains and vomiting, and Paul drove me to the hospital. Thank God for little things.

A handsome, loving, concerned, doctor who actually took an interest in his patients gave me the best news I'd ever heard – a real diagnosis. He told me I was having a gall bladder attack and I needed surgery. He wasn't a surgeon, but he gave me the name of a good surgeon he knew. He did not have to order all the other tests I'd had many times, but instead he just listened to what had happened to me over the years and he knew, he just knew. The next day after leaving the hospital I called the surgeon and to set up an appointment for three days later.

The doctor was an older gentleman, and we were told he was an excellent surgeon. After going through my history and looking over the X-rays and medicines I'd been given over the years, he told us there would be a fifty-fifty chance that an inflamed gall bladder was really what I had. I had been in so much pain I welcomed the chance for him to cut me open and check. He was the only one who wanted to take a chance. I said to him, "Please go in, do anything, and while I'm cut open can you please take out my appendix?" He stated if everything looked fine with my appendix he would not take it out because of the risk of other infections. I agreed with anything, just urging him to please do in the surgery. A surgery date was set for the next week. I was so excited for many reasons. One reason was that soon I would discover that I really might have something wrong with me and that it wasn't "just nerves," and there was a doctor willing to take a chance and go in to explore, and two, I now had hope that soon I could start feeling like a real person again.

On the morning of the surgery I was prepped, my stomach was washed with iodine, and I was sent down to the OR. When the surgeon lifted up my gown to check my stomach he shouted, "What in the world?" My stomach was covered in hives from the iodine and he didn't want to perform the surgery until that was cleared up. I told him I didn't care what happened or what it looked like, I just wanted him to do the surgery. That was the first time I ever broke out in hives from iodine. He laughed and went on with the IV drip to put me out.

I was told one hour after the surgery the doctor had called my husband and told him we had hit a home run. My gall bladder was diseased and there was brown sludge all around it, which was running into my liver and my spleen. If I had continued going on the way I was, I probably would have been dead in one year. My entire body had become septic from this brown sludge. It was a day to remember. The one bad thing was my appendix was fine so he left it in. Six months later I had appendicitis and was back in the surgery room once again. It was funny, I couldn't get anyone to open me up before to check me. Now I'd had two major surgeries six months apart.

Those days were great because now I had two problems down and one to go. The dizziness was far advanced now. I went to an ENT doctor (ears, nose, and throat), who referred me to a specialist at Emory University. He could not give me a diagnosis until we went through all the tests he was ordering for me. I was admitted into Emory where I was given all types of tests on my eyes in the front, back, and inside. There were tests where they would put water in my ears, spin me around, and check the size and shape of my pupils. Tests were run on my head up my nose and in my hair. One test the doctor wanted was a spinal tap that was to be performed by one of the students. The numbing solutions were put in my spine with no problems, but when he went to collect the fluid from my spine he missed, hit a nerve, and my leg went completely numb. The pain from my back was so excruciating I screamed for him to get the needle out of my back and get out of the room. The doctor apologized and asked if he could do the spinal tap instead. I told him under no circumstances would anyone touch me back there again. Other tests were completed and the diagnosis was brought in. It seemed I had a build-up of fluid in the right side of my head, and it was not able to drain properly so it kept building up and needed to come out. I had what is called Menieres Disease.

That was the cause of the ringing and double vision and the loss of hearing. What did I need to do to get rid of the fluid and all those sounds? Surgery, of course. I knew I wasn't nuts and complaining for nothing. Finally, I would be a totally new person again, whole and well.

The surgery date was set for two days later. The right side of my head was shaved down to the scull, a large line was cut from the side of the temple to the back by the ear. The fluid was removed and stitches were placed in my head. I did not want to stay in the hospital and asked my doctor to please let me go home. I assured them I would come right back if something changed over night. I went home and my hearing came back that night and the dizziness was gone. I continue to have some slight symptoms of dizziness when the weather changes and occasional ringing in my ears, but I have no longer suffer with double vision, and now when I get a little dizzy I know how to handle it. I am able to fly anywhere and we have been on eight cruises.

One day a few years later, while I was at work I started to hemorrhage and didn't know what was wrong. When I went to the doctor again, this time I learned I had endometriosis and another surgery would be necessary. So I had the surgery and now I am missing more parts of my body. The only lasting result from that surgery was hot flashes. I am still waiting for them to depart and go away! I am trying to eat right most of the time, exercise some of the time, and resting as much as I can some of the time.

Things went well for a short time. One afternoon in 1999 Paul and I went out to eat lunch at a place where we had never eaten before. Afterwards, while we were out shopping all of a sudden my face went numb. At first I couldn't speak and didn't know where I was. I told Paul how strange I felt. Maybe it was the new type of food I'd just eaten. My head started feeling very strange and for a second I couldn't focus. We were there to buy dining room chairs and we had to pass them on the way out. I told Paul to just pick up four chairs and then we needed to go home. He looked at me as if I had gone totally mad. We bought the chairs and went straight home.

I rested, but my mouth and face were still numb. I waited throughout the weekend to see if anything new developed, and on Monday my boss was so concerned that he sent me to the ER. After completing tests I was told I'd had a stroke. I was very lucky that it wasn't any worse. The look on my husband's face told me how frustrated he was that I'd waited all weekend to finally get to the hospital. A neurologist came in to examine me further and I was given medicine to take and was told to make an appointment to see him in his office the following week.

Things went well for a year, and then I had another stroke on the other side of my face. It seems at certain times my blood pressure drops too low and the skipping of heartbeats clots my blood, which then causes a stroke. Now I was numb on the other side of my face and nose. I was able to do well with that stroke also.

One year Paul and I went on a cruise to the Mediterranean for fourteen days. While the ship was docked we ate in Egypt at a five-star palace. Half the ship's passengers got food poisoning. Guess which half I was in? I couldn't believe it. I had watched so carefully what I had eaten. The next day we arrived in Greece, a country I had been waiting all my life to visit. I was determined to go sightseeing no matter how I felt. Paul and I did not go with the rest of the passengers on the tour guide buses. We hired a taxi for ourselves and had someone from the ship explain my problem with my food poisoning and having diarrhea. We asked if it was possible whenever I would yell "bathroom!" he could get me to one quickly, and he said yes. We only had to stop three times. I saw Greece, I took pictures in Greece, I stepped on the ground in Greece, and visited a few shops. I had accomplished my heart's desire in seeing Greece, and now I didn't care if we had to go home.

While I was at work one day in 2002, the side of my face went numb, again with loss of speech. I was taken to the ER again, more tests were run, and it was determined that I'd had my third stroke in four years. The only problem I have now is that my mouth is numb in certain areas. There is a slightly numb feeling on one side of my nose, and my memory is not all it used to be. I sometimes have difficulty giving answers to questions when people want those answers quickly. I have noticed that people run out of patience with me quickly.

Things went along smoothly with my health for about three years, and then guess what happened while we were attending a retreat? Once again I suffered a horrendous bout of food poisoning. The baked chicken was not baked enough. On Saturday two hours after eating I started with the vomiting, diarrhea, sweats, and chills. It lasted all evening without stopping. Sunday morning we left early to go home. On the way home I told Paul I needed the ER. As he drove up to the entrance I passed out. I was told they couldn't find a pulse. Someone grabbed me out of the car, threw me onto a gurney, started IVs and finally a small pulse started again. I was told it was probably a stomach flu and was sent home. For another two days all the symptoms continued. Paul took me to our family doctor, who gave me pain medicine and said I probably still had the flu. Again I was sent home, and he said if I became worse, to call him.

Naturally I continued to get worse so I called him. The doctor told me to take more pain medicine. The next day Paul had to go out of town and my mother came to stay with me. I was now starting to have dark black to green diarrhea. When my mom arrived there was no color in my face and I couldn't talk. She gave me the phone in the living room, and I called 911 and passed out. The ambulance came immediately and drove us to the hospital. Our wonderful neighbors came to stay with the dogs. They were so kind to us and slept at our home all week to care for the dogs. They are a true blessing. I was given the same medicine that cancer patients are given to help them stop vomiting after chemo treatments. I was admitted and given tests, as well as large dosages of potassium intravenously, of which I was severely depleted. After three days when my stools became dark green, the cultures showed that I had salmonella. Again my medicines were changed. This time an infectious disease doctor showed up. My mom stayed and slept at the hospital with me the entire time. She was there to help feed me, and she helped when I needed to go to the bathroom. I was very unsteady on my feet and wasn't allowed to go by myself. Mom was a blessing again in every way possible. I couldn't have asked for a better nurse. Stacy, our daughter, came every other day to take Mom to my house so that she could shower, change clothes, and rest a little. I was given strong medicines and kept in the hospital for one week, and finally after ten full weeks the salmonella poisoning was gone. Paul had been gone on a business trip the entire time I was in the hospital.

Today I am so glad to be alive, seeing our daughter grown with three children of her own, and spending more time with Paul and our dogs. God has truly been good to us. Paul's work still keeps him traveling often, but now I am able to stay by myself and function as a fairly normal person.

Throughout all my years of pain, heartaches, and not understanding why I had to go through these agonizing health problems, I never hated God; I just didn't understand Him. It was hard to not hate Him, but I knew deep down in my heart God always loved me then and He still loves me now.

My Child

My child, I have taken you this far,
To be humble, faithful, and true.
Don't let man's blindness corrupt you,
In whatever you say and do.

I have not taken you this far to stumble,
To walk in the shadows of man.
My mercy, my love, and direction,
Is what you'll follow — it's part of My plan.

My love for you is genuine,
Never fearful, with anguish or pain.
Just hear My voice and obey me,
Nothing to lose, but everything to gain.

Be silent; don't argue or run wild,
There's much work I need you to do.
Overlooking from the mountain we walked up,
Knowing unbelievers are waiting for you.

Stop worrying so much what you'll do,
Stop worrying so much what you'll say.
Hold on to My strength and protection,
I'll be with you each moment of each day.

Merle Debra
Written at the cabin — 1998

Chapter 6

Once Again "He" Has Spared My Life

By now you are probably wondering how many lives I have left.

During my teen years our family belonged to a beach club about thirty miles from our home. The grounds were kept quite nice with beautiful flowers, and the staff always kept the members in style with valet parking. As you entered through the clubhouse or the dining area there were large, full-length glass windows looking out to the inside of the beach club. The clubhouse dining room served breakfast, lunch, and dinner. The food was always served on beautiful, expensive china. There was a winding stairway that led to a cement path, which wound its way around to the pools. There were three swimming pools situated close to one another. In between the two adult pools there were lounge chairs to relax on. The third pool was for the little ones, and there were chairs for the moms to sit and watch. Down the stairs to the right of the club was the snack bar where we could buy hamburgers, hot dogs, ice cream, and all the junk food we could eat.

As you walked down on the right side there were two tennis courts, and next to those were two racquetball courts. Down at the far end of the club was the Long Island Sound. The water was beautiful for swimming, boating, or to just gaze out at while lying on the white sand. There was a snack bar where they served hot food. Past the ball courts and up a little grass hill were large and small cabanas. In the cabanas were changing rooms and an area where club members could leave their chairs and tables. When it rained there was enough room to have friends inside and for the adults and kids to play cards, games, or just sit and wait for the rain to stop.

Down towards the beach, and close enough to one of the pools, there was also a large, wide-open grassy area where we would sunbathe. Off to the right side of the club was a cement area where the mothers and fathers would play cards and mahjong, because it was shaded.

The beach club kept a busy schedule, and there was always something to do. On Monday evenings the club was quiet. On Tuesday evenings they held the young adults' movie night outdoors. Wednesday evening was game night. Thursday evening was teen party night. On Saturday nights the adults came to drink, dance, and party. Sunday evening was family night. I can't remember Friday nights because that was always my date night.

One hot summer afternoon I was playing racquetball with some friends on the back court. In the front court my dad was playing very competitively as he did all day with his friends. I was in the back end waiting for the ball to be hit when all of a sudden a racket came flying backwards and hit me right in the middle of my throat. At that time the rackets where made of solid wood around three inches in thickness, with large holes in the center and a wrist band that should have been on the opponent's arm. Unfortunately, in this instance, the handle was not on their wrist and their racket came flying backwards into my neck.I screamed, lost my voice, and ran to my dad in the front court. I tried to talk and showed him what happened. He told me to go to my mother and said I would be fine. He was too busy playing racquetball and didn't want to be disturbed. I ran to my mom with my other friends and they told her what happened. She sat me down and called my dad. I was in the car in a wet bathing suit, being driven to the doctors.

The next thing I knew I was being carried quickly to the car and was driven to an ear, nose, and throat doctor. The doctor sat me in a chair, sprayed something down my throat, and inserted a long metal mirror, telling me to keep swallowing it until it reached my vocal cords. I started to panic. He calmed me down slightly and said it had to be done, so I should try and relax. When the mirror finally made its way out, the look on the doctor's face was not a look of good tidings. He smiled that smile when something is wrong and asked if he could speak with my mom in the next room. After returning, the doctor told me what had happened and gave me a set of instructions. I was to listen very carefully and do everything he told me to do. It seemed when the racket hit my throat it formed a blood clot on my vocal cords. If I was to scream or get excited it would rupture and I would die. The look on my mother's face was worse than the doctor's. Now I started to get nervous. My instructions were to relax with no screaming or talking, not one single word. Anything I needed was to be written down. I was not to sleep flat on my back in case my nose would drip, and I had to try not to ever sneeze, as there may be a chance the clot could rupture. The foods would have to be neither hot nor cold. The food was to be the consistency of baby food with no chewing. I could eat very soft, room temperature apple sauce, peaches, a lot of Jell-O, and plenty of room temperature liquids.

Early every morning I had a standard appointment to come into the doctor's office where I had to swallow the mirror down my throat to check my progress. The answer was the same every day: no leakage, it was not growing, keep up the good work, see you tomorrow. This went on for two weeks. Finally, the day came. As the doctor drew the mirror out of my throat, he gave me a piece of bubble gum and told me to blow the biggest bubble I possibly could. I was so scared, but he was the doctor and I prayed he knew what he was asking me to do. I chewed the gum for minute to work it to the right consistency, and then blew a big bubble. After it popped the doctor asked me what my name was and said I was to answer him.

I could talk! I went in one more time after that day for my last checkup, But that day I received a clean bill of health, finally.

My dad did feel sorry for me and apologized for ignoring me and telling me to go away. Since then I have never stepped foot on a racquetball court. Can you blame me?

She was a 1983 maroon Buick Regal, my love of a car — my first very own car. She was beautiful and I tried to always keep her looking fine. Although I loved this car like she was brand new, she was getting up in years. The heater worked but did not blow out warm air, and the air conditioner stopped working altogether. The windows did go up and down, all the mirrors were still intact, and she still looked fine, but on the outside only. No one could believe at thirteen years old she only had fifty thousand miles on her. The car was used for work and to run occasional errands. I felt safe in my Buick because of her size. She was big and made out of heavy metal. Even at her age she still purred like new.

One morning I was one block away from work. I had my sunglasses on the bridge of my nose, and on the front seat next to me was a cake I'd made for work, while in the back seat were papers in a neat stack. I approached an intersection where I had the green light and the oncoming cars had a yield green sign to make their left-hand turn across my lane. Just as I was passing through the intersection one of those left-turning cars did not yield to my right-of-way and bang, slammed straight into my car. Seconds before they rammed into my I yelled "Jesus!" as loud as I could, and in that second I passed out. My car was hit in the front, which pushed the motor straight back into the body of the car. My door was completely smashed and the car was totaled. I remember after a few seconds I heard sirens, and ambulances were gathered to the front and side of my car. The police tried to help get me out of my side of the car, but my door was locked; my window was cracked opened enough to get an arm through it, so the men wanted to crowbar me out. I had just awakened from passing out when on the passenger side of the car a fireman yelled to the policeman standing on my side to just reach in and unlock the door. He smiled and opened the door.

When I began to look around, I realized my glasses were still on my face in the same place on my nose, and my cake still sat on the seat next to me. It had not even been thrown from side to side or front wards; it was still sitting in the same spot where I had placed it. The papers remained in their stack unmoved. The front glass was never broken and the mirrors were never cracked, but the entire front of the car was pushed in. When I was taken from the car there were red stains on my scrubs. The woman in the ambulance was about to cut my pants open to check for blood, but I yelled, "Don't cut my scrubs, do you know how much they cost?" The red stains were the red from the inside of my steering wheel where my leg had been caught.

"This one is a live one. She seems fine to me, worrying about us cutting her pant leg," one of the nurses called out as she laughed.

I was then put on the gurney and wrapped with a back and neck brace. As I looked to the side I saw and heard the man in the other car telling the police he was wrong and should not have tried to go through the light. His car was also totaled.

I was taken to the hospital, and the first person I saw was my son-in-law. Greg is a police officer in the county where I had my accident. He was the first one they called. He in turn called my husband. I was so happy to see his smile and know I was still alive. After having many X-rays the results were in. I had not one broken bone, not one tear in any part of my skin, not one visible bruise. I did have a slight concussion, very sore bones, neck pain, and stiffness in my joints.

Two days later I went to my Doctor of Osteopath, who adjusted my entire body, especially my neck and legs. I believe if he hadn't adjusted me I possibly could still be having some stiffness and joint problems to this day. After being adjusted, I tried to step off the table to the floor, but I passed out for a few seconds, probably from the pain. I am thankful for his skill and ability in knowing where and how to manipulate the body. (Thank you again, doc!)

I believe with all my heart when I called out to Jesus He heard my cry and came to my aid. He sat with me when I passed out and held me to His breast. When I awoke I was not screaming nor was I afraid; I somehow sensed that now I had a different kind of peace than I'd ever experienced before in my life. I never saw any heavenly figures or white lights; I knew it was Jesus simply because *I knew*. He was with me. He really does treasure my life. He shielded me from danger, He kept me alive and in one piece, He never let any harm come my way. He loves me. He truly loves me and will protect me as long as I need Him. Thank you, Lord; You are my lifesaver.

Peace

You are my God, and I love You,
You're with me every night and day,
You are my God, and I love You,
You're here with me whenever I pray.

You're my God, my peace of mind.
You're my God, my peace of mind.

You came to me when I needed You most,
I cried for help and there You were.
You came into my heart, and blessed my soul,
And I love You, my Father, my God.

You're my God, my peace of mind.
You're my God, my peace of mind.

How could I question Your own words,
And doubt You wouldn't bring me peace.
You fill our souls, minds, and bodies,
Keep us blessed with Your own love.

You're my God, my peace of mind.
You're my God, my peace of mind.

Merle Debra
May, 1995

Chapter 7

I Want What She Has, But What Is It?

Finally, after nine and a half years, Paul was discharged from the army. Our family of four — myself, Paul, Stacy, and our dog Princess — moved to Roswell, Georgia. We found the perfect apartment to rent. In the complex there was a lake, plenty of areas to walk, a clubhouse and many children for Stacy to play with. Our rental had three rather large bedrooms, a large eat-in kitchen, a living room, and two bathrooms. Living on the bottom floor apartment, we had a small cement deck. It was convenient for walking Princess, and I was also able to grow a small patch of tomato plants. We were able to have two chairs and a small table, and I made a walkway to the side of the house that led to a grassy area where the school bus picked up and dropped off the children from school. Because we were so close to the stop, most of the time we had Stacy's friends over after school. The one and only problem was being on the ground level, which meant anyone could look through the windows.

My parents were always kind and generous to us when we needed them, so when my dad became ill and they needed help we felt it was only right to share our home with them. I was thankful the rooms were a pretty good size considering all the "stuff" we had all accumulated over the years.

How does one fit in with a different culture, from living up north for many years and now living in the south? You do as they do, or at least you try to.

My taste in clothes was somewhat different than what some of my new friends were wearing. I decided it wouldn't hurt for me to try and buy some skirts and dresses like they wore. Paul had to go to the Carolinas for work and I thought it would be great to go along with him. As we drove around we came to a cute area with many clothing shops, antique stores, and mom 'n pop restaurants specializing in southern cooking. We parked the car, and as I walked around the block I noticed a store with ladies' clothes in the window that were just what I needed to make a change. I bought four long skirts, two with large flower prints, one with ships, and one plain. The skirts I wore were always either slightly above or below the knee. The last time I had worn a long dress was at my junior prom dance. The shirts I bought that day had lace around the neck or around the sleeves. My shirts never had lace and it made me itch. My favorite colors are the dark-winter reds, blues, blacks, and browns. The colors of my new shirts were pastel. The sweaters had very

I'm A Jew I Don't Do Jesus

long sleeves and were high around the neck. Mine were short to the waist with a round collar. Now for the shoes, of course they matched the shirts. I can remember thinking, *Oh my goodness, whatever have I done?* I told Paul I would try them for a while to see if it would work for me. I tried, I really did try to wear those clothes for some time, but after awhile I had to go back to who I really am. The clothes had to go.

Acquiring a southern accent has also been interesting. I have been told by my daughter and some of my friends that I should not try to speak southern, because mine has too much of a northern twist to it. Thank you one and all. I have lived in Georgia since 1977, but I am still learning!

Georgia is where I met my friend Jimmie. Her husband was Paul's boss at the time when she and I first met. Jimmie is a soft-spoken, loving woman with not an enemy in the world. I had never met anyone like her before. I kept asking myself, *why is she so different? What does she have that I don't have?* Jimmy has a beautiful singing voice and she writes her own music. A few of the instruments she plays are the banjo, guitar, piano, and keyboard. Buddy, her bird, talks and sounds just like her. Buddy tells you he loves you and enjoys walking on the outside of his cage.

I enjoyed Jimmie's company and we started getting together regularly. We spent time sharing our lives with each other, told secrets like schoolgirls, laughed together and had the best times, when one day she asked me "the" question.

"Do you believe in Jesus?"

I looked at her and blurted out, "I'm a Jew, I don't do Jesus!"

At that point she smiled and shook her head slightly as if to say 'okay, I won't go there', and then she quickly changed the subject. She never seemed hurt or angry. I'm sure she was a little disappointed; nevertheless, she was always kind to me.

After popping "the" question, the church Jimmie was attending was rehearsing for a play to be given at Easter time. Jimmie was one of the cast members, so each day when she went to rehearsal she would ask her church friends to pray for her little Jewish friend. Jimmie never told them my name, only just to pray for 'her little Jewish friend'. Of course that secret was kept from me. I would not have understood at that time why they were praying for me and what it might have meant for me later on.

Jimmie and I started to get together more often and our friendship became closer. There was something about her that I loved. I wasn't sure what it was; I just knew I wanted what she had. We would go out to stores and shop for hours. People would tell her their life story and their pains, and she would pray for some of them right then and there, and for others she would tell them she'd keep them in her prayers. Standing next to her I would just smile. It always sounded pretty good to me; besides, what did I know then? No matter who it was they would warm up to her in no time. When they were ready to say goodbye, the other person would hug her and thank her. I was really impressed.

Jimmie always smiled, and she always spoke great things about everyone she knew. She always found something nice to say about everyone. To me, she doesn't have a mean bone in her body. When we would go shopping and the parking lots were full she would pray and ask the Lord to open one up for us, and we would get a space right in front. Other times even if it was the darkest, blackest day she would bring an umbrella so it wouldn't rain on our great day together, and it wouldn't. I love her love for her God. I never really paid much attention to God the way she did.

Growing up I knew God was there, but I never asked Him to do anything for me. I didn't know I could. I knew He was God and that was all I needed to know at that time in my life. Besides, what else would I need? If I wanted anything I could just go out and buy it. The only thing I could not buy was what Jimmie had, and I really wanted that. She had that one thing I could not put my finger on. How could someone be so happy all the time and not worry about anything? She would always say, "God will make a way; He will take care of everything." I would think sarcastically, *Oh really?!*

Spending so much time with Jimmie made me want more of what she had. Where could I find it? I was becoming very jealous. I wanted that kind of peace, gentleness, kindness, and most of all, the love that she shared with others, but where was it to be found?

For seven years Jimmie and her Christian friends continued to pray for her little Jewish friend.

I'll Come Again

I wish you could have been here,
The first time I walked my path.
There was love, peace, songs of joy,
But mostly, there was fear.

To follow me some had to die,
To end up in My kingdom.
While others lived in hell on earth,
To steal, to kill, and to lie.

I've taught My love, peace, and wisdom,
My parables, helped to learn.
While others thought My mind was twisted,
Yelling, "Stone him, kill him, let him burn!"

I've always walked in peace,
My Father kept me well.
I taught of all His promises,
The difference of heaven and hell.

One more time I'll come again,
My light and shining sword.
I'll ride with honor, glory and love,
King of kings, and Lord of lords.

Merle Debra

Chapter 8

The Night I Gave My Life to Yeshua

Tuesday, August 20, 1990: It was a night I will never forget.

Not far from my home was a Messianic Synagogue I had driven past many times. Not knowing what Messianic meant, I also had no desire to visit or check it out. I had no idea who attended, or even what or who these people were. During the holidays and occasionally on Saturdays I would meet my parents at the synagogue where they were members. I really did not have a desire to belong to any place of worship at that time in my life, and since Paul was not attending church, we stayed home on Saturdays and Sundays.

It was a warm summer evening and the sun was just starting to go down. I didn't have any plans for the evening, so when my close friend Jimmie called and asked if I wanted to go out, I said yes. I

I'm A Jew I Don't Do Jesus

had the greatest amount of trust in Jimmie because she'd earned that trust. I knew that if she said something would be fine, it would be fine. But this time I wasn't so sure it was a good idea to go where she wanted to go. She wanted to go to a place of worship and a Bible study being held at a Messianic Jewish Congregation, the same one I had driven past many times before. Most of the time I was not even aware of what went on in that place. This night I was going to find out.

I received a phone call from another Jewish friend asking what I was doing that night. I told her where Jimmie and I were going and she told me she would like to join us. They both came to my home first and we all drove in one car.

As we approached the front door, I felt calm, but I didn't know what to expect. I decided to be brave and just open the doors. We breezed confidently straight through the next set of open double doors and walked right up to the second front row and took our seats. At that moment I could not have told you what the room looked like or who was around me. I felt comfortable in the sense there were no crosses or any statues hanging on the walls. It was very Jewish. I saw the ark with the Torah inside with a light above it that burns continually. In the pews were the prayer books with Hebrew written on one side of the page and English on the other. *This is a Jewish place,* I thought with slight amazement, *not like any synagogue I have ever been in, but still, it is Jewish.* For the time being I felt all right.

I'm A Jew I Don't Do Jesus

The pews started to fill up with adults while the children went to their own Bible study group downstairs in the building. If the rabbi gave a message that night I have no idea what the topic was. I felt as if I was in a bubble looking out while others were talking, but I heard no voices. Before I realized it, the rabbi was finished with his Bible study. I heard people talking and laughing, and I watched them shaking hands with everyone around them. The children entered the sanctuary and joined their parents.

The rabbi was standing down in front of the pews between the two aisles. Three men came down the center aisle to the rabbi. One gentleman was carrying a large round bowl filled with small pieces of matzo. The other two men each carried a large platter with some small clear plastic cups. One set of glasses was filled with wine, and the other set was filled with grape juice.

Before I knew it, row by row, each person stood up and made their way to the center aisle to form two lines. The men, women, and children, one by one, came down the aisle to receive one piece of matzo and one glass of either wine or juice. After receiving, everyone went back to their seats. They were all smiling, happy, and ready to do their part. The children didn't need to be told what to do; they already knew. If they knew, then why didn't I? My Jewish friend and I looked at each other clueless. The two of us just sat in our pews and looked around. We could not go with the rest of the congregation because we had no idea what to do. Jimmie was sitting on my right. All of a sudden she stood up, excused herself, and went to receive the matzo and wine. Usually I would follow Jimmie, but this time was not the right time. She knew what to do and was happy to join in. My Jewish friend and I remained in our seats. She also had no idea of what was happening.

Suddenly I began crying. I didn't understand why I could not go and participate with them. I felt so lost. The congregation was now standing as they waited for the next step in the ceremony with smiles on their faces. This was good and they were happy. Looking around at their faces I was now sobbing.

The rabbi read a prayer for the bread in Hebrew and then in English. After the prayer the congregation ate of the bread. Following the first prayer a second prayer was prayed for the wine, again in Hebrew and English. This time they drank the wine or grape juice. As I listened to the prayers, I realized they were the ones I had heard and said for many years in all the synagogues I had attended. They were prayers that were said with the start of the Friday Sabbath every weekend. In other temples, at the end of the service, the rabbi would either go to the back of the room by the door, while other rabbis would stand in the front of the sanctuary. They would say a prayer for the wine then take a sip, then say the prayer for the bread. As the congregation left the sanctuary each person could take a piece of the bread. I was almost shaking from crying so much.

When the service finished, a young, very sweet woman came from behind me. She touched me so softly on my shoulder and whispered in my ear, saying, "I know what you need." I said to myself,

How does she know what I need? I don't even know what I need. She took my hand and guided me to the back of the sanctuary where the rabbi was talking with some other women. My friend Jimmie and my other friend were right behind me. The rabbi, myself, Jimmie, the young woman and one other woman stood in the back of the room. We all held hands and formed a circle. I was standing next to the rabbi, and I heard him say, "Repeat after me the same words I say." At that time I had no idea why I had to do this. *Why do I have to repeat what he was saying? What does it all mean?* It happened so fast I didn't know what hit me. I felt very uncomfortable. While the rabbi spoke he kept pulling me towards him and I kept pulling away from him. I didn't understand nor did I want to be there with these people saying words I didn't want to say. I didn't understand why I had to repeat the words. Nevertheless, I did repeat some of them, and everyone standing around had smiles on their faces, gave me a hug, and the rabbi invited me to come back and visit. My mind was reeling with questions. *What just happened and why did I have to do what I just did?* I couldn't wait to get out of there and go home, home where I felt safe.

Jimmie and my other friend and I came back to my home. I still didn't know what had just happened. Not only did I not understand what happened in that service, I did not know what happened afterwards. Now I was more confused than before. I put together a plate of cookies and we all had something to drink. I was standing with my back to the sink and started to cry again. Jimmie came over to me and stood in front of me.

She put her hand on my shoulder and asked, "What's wrong, Merle?"

I replied tearfully, "I felt upset that I could not go take the wine and bread with the rest of you. I felt left out, Jimmie, but I don't even know why. Whenever I've been in a regular temple I've always been able to eat the bread, so why not tonight? What were they were doing anyway?" It wasn't that the tradition or custom was strange to me, but rather it was the way the others had participated in it that had me baffled.

Jimmie smiled and explained what communion is, what it signifies in the Bible, and why we pray the way we pray and partake of the blessings. This was a totally different meaning of bread and wine than I had ever heard. She was so knowledgeable and excellent at explaining Bible stories. Jimmie has known her personal Lord and Savior for many years and has a solid understanding of Bible stories and verses.

Jimmy prayed prayers ever so softly, not demanding, and I trusted her in all she said and the way she presented herself to others. I was sobbing and had no idea why this was happening to me. Before this evening we'd had many other conversations about the Bible, and I was in love with the book of Matthew.

I turned to face the sink as the water was running. I was washing my hands and crying all at the same time when I heard Jimmy ask me in her sweet, low voice, "Do you want to receive Jesus into your heart?"

I said, "Yes I do."

My other friend was sitting at the kitchen table watching, never making a comment and not really wanting to be a part of this.

Jimmie asked me to close my eyes. I trusted Jimmie with all my heart so I did as she said. She held my hands in hers, I closed my eyes, and then she told me about Jesus and His coming to earth, and why He came for me and died for me. I was told about salvation, prayers, His death and crucifixion, and His love for me.

She explained how my heavenly Father would take care of me and love me like no one has ever loved me. She talked about the trinity of the Father, Son, and Holy Spirit. She said I could receive the same peace, kindness and love that she had. She explained that of all the sins I have ever committed in my life, Yeshua has cleansed me of them. I was told how much He loved me, and now, I could start a new life in Him. Did I want this? You bet I did, and more. She led me into a beautiful prayer of repentance and of accepting Jesus, Yeshua, my Messiah, into my heart and my new life. I could feel my heart pounding. Then she touched my head ever so softly with her hands and I felt a hot, fiery feeling come down onto my head, flow down into my body, and travel to the bottom of my feet. I felt on fire, hot to the touch, and my face was bright red and my ears were glowing. It was the most wonderful and yet shocking feeling.

One other time Jimmie came to my house when I had a cold and asked if I wanted prayer for my illness. I loved to hear her pray and again, I trusted her. We went into the living room, pulled a turquoise chair in front of my fireplace, and sat down. Jimmie came and stood in back of me and placed her hands on my head. While my eyes were closed she prayed, and a warm sensation spread from the top of my head down to my toes. It was so wonderful, I almost did not want it to stop. My cold became much better immediately. That was exciting to me. I have always been open to listen to Jimmie and hear what she has to say because she speaks truth.

This night the heat of my accepting Jesus felt much hotter and lasted much longer. There were no bells going off, no choir of angels singing, no lightning from the sky, no yelling or screaming. It was a wonderful, peaceful, warm, gentle feeling. I opened my eyes and it felt as if I had been in my own world. She smiled and asked how I felt. There was a special softness in my heart.

My lips started moving and some words were trying to come out, but somehow I couldn't understand what I was trying to say.

Jimmie asked, "Do you want a prayer language of your own to use to pray to God?"

I replied, "Of course I do! I want all there is to receive."

I was told to close my eyes again and once again Jimmie started to pray. She prayed a very simple prayer to God for my prayer language to be given to me. It was explained to me that this was my evening of telling Yeshua "yes," and that I needed Him and wanted Him to work in my life from that moment forward, and that He would use me however He sees fit. Jimmie told me just to keep pouring out my heart to God, and to keep letting the words just flow out. They did flow out, and when I heard them I realized I'd just received from God a brand-new prayer language, and it was awesome. It is a way the Lord and I speak to each other. I do not understand what is being said, but God does. I felt as if a burden had been lifted off me and I was now a child of God. I was now like Jimmie. I felt like jumping up and down.

I accepted Yeshua in front of the sink while the water was slightly running. My prayer language was also given to me in front of the sink. I believe God knew I would be relaxed by the water and things would seem easier for me. I believe God knows what we need at the right time, in the right place, to receive whatever He has to give us when we are willing to accept it.

The water relaxes me and helps my mind get into a peaceful mode. Since I grew up by the water and we have taken all our vacations at beaches, God knew in His wonderful sense of humor that if He put me near the water I would listen. My other girlfriend didn't know what to think of all of this. When asked, she replied this was not what she wanted in her life right now. It was getting late and my other girlfriend wanted out, but I didn't want Jimmie to leave. I had so many other questions I wanted to ask her, but because the time was getting late and they had come over in different cars, Jimmie had to leave as well.

Paul had been upstairs all that evening and never heard a word of what had happened right below him in the kitchen. That evening I never said a word to Paul about what had happened between me, Jimmie, and my new life with Yeshua.

After my guests left I immediately went into the bathroom to take a shower. The joy and excitement I felt came pouring out in prayers and praises, both spoken and sung with much laughter. I was so excited I couldn't stand it. I cupped my hands around my mouth and starting praying very softly in my prayer language to the Lord. I had so much to tell the Lord, but I wasn't sure how to express myself. I had prayers for my husband, family, friends, thanksgivings for my life, and so many other things, but I didn't know the right words to pray. Here I was a new, a very new believer, and I wanted to save the world that night. I felt as if I was bouncing off spongy walls, and I wanted to call everyone I knew to tell them what had happened to me that evening.

I was beginning to feel afraid I would not know how to pray in the morning. All through the night I kept getting up, cupping my hands around my mouth, praying in English and in my prayer language. I asked God, *Are You still there for me? Can You really hear my prayers? Will You walk with me in times of trouble, especially when I tell others how I accepted Yeshua the previous evening? What will my family say or do? Lord, will You protect me when my parents yell and scream about my decision? Will my parents want to disown me?*

I had so many questions without any answers, and for the first time I became afraid.

My Husband, My Lover, My Friend

Have I told you, how proud of whom you've become,
My husband, my lover, my friend?
Through thick and thin, pain and sorrow,
There's been nothing that you can't mend.

Our years together we've had trials,
Only to teach us each day of our strength.
Together we've been able to conquer them,
Because for you, there's no measure nor length

My love is far deeper than oceans and seas,
Listen quietly, you'll hear my voice.
My heart for you is always opened,
Forever, you'll have the keys.

Remember, I love you so deeply,
All my brokenness you've been able to mend.
Remember, no matter how far apart we are,
You're my husband, my lover, my friend.

Merle Debra

Chapter 9

First to the Jew, Then to the Gentile

As soon as I awoke in the morning, I started praying. *Hello God, are you still there? Thank You for loving me. Will You be with me today?*

It was very early, but I was still so excited that I just had to call Jimmie. I thanked her for a blessed evening and helping me find a new life, and I told her how I kept waking up all throughout the night praying. I was happy that my prayer language to God was still with me. The little chuckle in her voice was an indication of how she was trying not to laugh. My dear friend and I discussed my becoming a new believer, a follower of Yeshua and what it meant from now on. She also told me not to worry, because He, my heavenly Father, would not take away my prayer language.

Jimmie had great advice concerning Paul. From past experience she had with other new believers, she wanted to help me handle myself when discussing the Bible and Yeshua with my husband.

The things I should not do would be:

—Do not constantly talk, nag, or try to change his views.
—Try not to force my views on him and be careful not to jump down his throat too fast.
—Remember that if I try to control or condemn him about reading the Bible he may turn the other way.
—Do not sound like a raving maniac, flying by the seat of my pants.

Her positive suggestions were:

—Go easy on him and remember that I was in his shoes not too long ago.
—Let Paul see me enjoying reading the Bible, walking softly before him and the Lord, and just showing him love, mine as well as Yeshua's love.

It is the power of God for the salvation of everyone who believes, first for the Jew, then for the Gentile (Romans 1:16).

I started watching as many Christian television stations as I could. I was so hungry to learn more about the Bible. When Paul would walk into the bedroom I would quickly switch the station to another channel. I didn't want him to feel I was trying to push Jesus on him, especially if he was not ready. I didn't want to push him away, either, so I tried to be gentle about my new beliefs. When I had questions about things I had just read, I would ask Paul if he knew anything about that subject. These were topics such as the Holy Spirit, talking in tongues, a prayer language, and some of the things Yeshua said and did. Paul had gone to a Catholic high school and had attended Wednesday afternoons and Sunday mornings in church. I thought he had read the Bible and knew some of the Bible characters and stories. Every time I asked Paul questions, I could see the wheels start spinning in his mind. He wasn't sure of any of the answers. I believe that was when he began searching. Every once in awhile I would see Paul reading his Bible, taking notes, and watching less and less of his regular television shows. It was happening; Paul was becoming inquisitive. Occasionally he would come to me with an answer to one of my questions, and when he did I would become excited, but I had to remember I still needed much patience and not to push him too quickly.

It was not much longer after the evening of my new birth when my parents came to our home. They knew right off the bat something was very different about me. One drastic change my parents' and Paul noticed was that I did not curse or use the Lord's name in vain, which had been a very large part of my conversation before. For many years I had a mouth like a truck driver. (No offense to any truck or bus driver; that was an expression used years ago when I lived in New York.) I never let on to my parents

I had accepted Yeshua into my heart and life. They just knew something was different. I left Bibles and different kinds of books around the house. I was also trying to clean up my act as a wife and friend. It takes time, work, and patience to change habits that have been part of your life for years, and therefore I am still a work in progress. Even today I am still careful with my actions and words with Paul.

My parents realized I had become one of "them," and neither parent wanted to talk to me. They believed I had converted and given up being Jewish. It was a death to them. They wanted nothing to do with me and they didn't want to visit us any longer. I tried to explain I was born Jewish and I would die Jewish, and that I was still Jewish — in fact, more Jewish than before. That made them even angrier. How would they be able to explain me and what I had become to their friends? Mom was uncomfortable to even have me in her synagogue. She was afraid I would tell someone what I had done.

I started attending the Messianic Congregation by myself. I had never heard such beautiful music. It was so alive. It began filling a hole I had in my heart. I was now one of those happy people who could go down the aisle, stand in line, receive my bread and wine, say the prayers, and partake of holy communion. If I cried, it was of happiness, not out of sadness. I attended every Friday evening for one year. I made some wonderful friends, and I hoped that someday Paul would become just a little jealous for what I had. I could see he was starting to, but in my heart I wanted it to happen now. I was starting on a new chapter of my life with new friends and happy times, and it didn't seem right that he was not involved in it. But gradually he was starting to change; I could see it. I continued to attend synagogue on Friday evenings feeling lonely without Paul. During the services we prayed, sang, had fellowship, heard a sermon, and worshiped our loving God.

One day I was praying, *God, why isn't Paul ready? What is taking him so long? For one year I have felt lonely attending synagogue by myself. I watch all the husbands, wives and children together having a wonderful time. Please God, I want to be able to attend services with Paul. If it is the only way we can worship together, I will even go to a church. That is not my heart's desire, Lord, but for the sake of being with Paul I would go.* I thought about what I had asked, and afterwards I went back to God and prayed, *I know what I said earlier in my prayer, Lord, but in my heart I was only pleading out of desperation; please, not a church!*

One Friday evening I went to services as usual. I came home and, as it was late, I went right to sleep. The next morning as I was waking up, Paul came into the bedroom, walked over to my side of our bed, and said, "I think I would like to go to synagogue services this morning." My first reaction was surprise, but inside I was so happy.

I told him, "Wait for me, I'm coming." I jumped up, showered, dressed, and out the door we went. I didn't want to miss this day for anything. Our drive was not even a full two minutes. I was so excited that we would be walking together into a synagogue, not a church. I thanked God a thousand times for this special answer to prayer.

As we walked through the front door, Paul said, "It feels like home."

I asked myself, *What just happened?* I remember thinking, *I'm the Jewish one; I have been attending here for a year. Why don't I feel the same? Why does this not feel like my home?* I guess I had taken all my happiness for granted. Maybe it felt like home and I never realized it. The men of the synagogue immediately loved Paul. Since I had been attending all year and my friends knew and prayed for Paul, they were excited to see him with me that morning. Paul had an instant family, a start of peace on earth, good will to men. Once again, God's timing was perfect.

It was a wonderful feeling to be able to attend services with my spouse. We began reading the Bible, praying, and worshiping the Lord together. We know this must be pleasing to our Lord and Savior.

I thank Jimmie for her words of wisdom during that year while I was waiting for Paul to give his life over to the Lord. I was jealous and wanted what Jimmie had, and Paul became jealous of what I was experiencing. After we began to read and discuss the Bible together, it wasn't much longer before Paul became a believer and was baptized. He has since entered into the ministry. We Thank God for giving us tender hearts and willing minds.

Shortly after I became a believer there was a split in the church Jimmie and her husband were attending. Some of the congregation stayed at the church while one of the priests and most of her friends chose to leave. Some went to different churches while others formed their own church. There were others who started attending the Messianic Synagogue I was attending.

One evening I was in the ladies room talking with a friend about my friend Jimmie. Another woman overheard our conversation and asked how I knew Jimmie. I told her how we met and how I accepted Yeshua through Jimmie. She burst out laughing with joy and was so excited. She started screaming and waving her arms up and down and hugging me.

"You're Jimmie's little Jewish friend," she announced in between hugs. Noticing my baffled expression as I was thinking, *how do you know me?*, she explained how Jimmie would come into rehearsal every day asking for everyone to pray for her little Jewish friend. For seven years the church had continued to pray for me. Jimmie never told me she had asked anyone to pray for me. We came out of the bathroom hugging, laughing, shrieking with joy, and talking very loudly. To anyone who would listen she would point to me and tell them, "She's the one I have been praying about for seven years!" There were a few other people there from her other church so we went over to them, told them who I was, and then we were all jumping up and down shouting for joy with tears flowing. We couldn't wait to tell all the other prayer partners. I couldn't wait to call Jimmie and tell her I'd found out what she had done and how much I loved her and her patience and devotion to the Lord, as well as her willingness to be His messenger to me and her friends.

This was another night of celebration and the beginning of a new and wonderful relationship in the Lord. He had this time and this night all picked out for all of us. I wished Jimmie had been there, because she was the reason for all that had happened. Just think what might've happened to me if Jimmie had not been faithful to listen to the Lord and offer His words of salvation to all who will listen, even a "little Jewish girl." Who knows where I would be now!

Praise, Promise, and My Vow

I thank You, Lord, for Your prophetic words,
For others to know You're real.
The visions, dreams, and interpretations,
To bring them closer to how You feel.

I promise to keep Your name Holy,
To honor You in every way.
Lifting up hands with praise and admiration,
And in everything I do and say.

I confess I don't always share You,
It's not that I am ashamed.
My boldness is in my actions and mouth,
To those who despise Your name.

Lord, help me to be a witness,
That's my life's everlasting goal.
To never deny my love for You,
And to reach every living soul.

Merle Debra

Chapter 10

The First Time I Thought I Could Help

Through His Word, God has taught us to love our neighbors as ourselves and to help those less fortunate when needed. If they are hungry, we are to give them food to eat, and when they are without shelter, we should give them a place to stay. However, God also wants us to use the common sense He has given us to use.

I was trying to figure out all the plans by myself. I thought I could figure out all the work and how I would be successful in the end. By relying on myself alone, I had opened the door wide open for failure, and then I had stepped in that door and walked across the threshold into disaster.

The character traits God wants us to show our brothers and sisters are: kindness, gentleness, meekness, patience, and love, which is the most important one.

Before I realized it I seemed to have lost all meekness and kindness, and where was my love hiding? It was not that I didn't try. I tried with all my heart. Unfortunately, it was not with the heart of the Father. Many times my patience became my worst enemy. My lack of love for others was turning into pure hatred, which is not healthy for anyone.

Love is patient, love is kind. It does not envy, it does not boast, it is not proud (1Corinthians 13:4).

During the late 1980s one of my family members was having a difficult time in her life. She had gone through a difficult divorce, and even though she had full custody of their two sons, the boys had finished school and gone on to college. Her sons seemed to be fine but their mother was not. No matter what she tried she could not get ahead financially, and her life seemed to be going nowhere. She needed help. Could Paul and I be her help? I had the thought that Paul and I could bring her here to live with us and help give her a new start in life. Paul and I prayed and believed it would be a good idea.

Our plan was to help her start with a fresh, new chapter in her life, surrounded by the peaceful atmosphere in our home. By this time our daughter, Stacy, was grown and married with three children of her own. Paul and I were in agreement and so it was settled; we would bring Sharon here to our home. I really wanted to help her.

My desire was that we could become friends and just pour love on her. I felt deeply sad for the way things turned out for her. She had such sadness, hurt, and confusion of how and where the rest of her life was to end up. Paul and I had the means to help her. All we wanted to do was to bless her. We wanted her to be free from worry about money, food, or shelter. Paul and I thought she would come to live with us, get a job, and earn enough money to eventually be able to support herself, get her own apartment, or even buy a home. We had absolutely no ulterior motive but to be loving and giving. We just wanted to help. Our home was large enough for the three of us to live comfortably without stepping on one another. Because of her lack of money, we felt it would cause her undue stress if we asked her for any help financially with the added expenses of having a third person in our home.

At the time Paul was using one of our comfortable large rooms downstairs as his office. Computers, phones, desks, faxes, and shelves were all lined around the room. Now we would have to squeeze them all into a smaller area upstairs. Paul was willing to do whatever it would take to make life easier for all of us. He really is an amazing gentleman. Paul never complains about anything. He is easygoing and has a heart big enough to fill the whole earth. After moving the office upstairs, our basement was now ready for its new renovation.

Building furniture and fixing broken items are a few of Paul's hobbies, only this project was too big even for him. We hired a contractor and the renovation started. Next to his office was a storage room. We cut it in half and put up a wall. We knocked out a portion of the wall facing his office to make a doorway leading to a new bathroom. We added a full white marble bathroom, with marble white cabinets and shelves. We installed large white tiles on the floor and a large glass white marble corner shower. There wasn't a window in the bathroom so we added lights to make it brighter.

Adjoining Paul's office was another large room that was used as a living room. We pulled up the old carpeting and laid down a light, white carpeting. For some of us, white carpet tends to be a big mistake, but it made the rooms appear brighter and wider.

There was a window in this room with a large sliding glass door which led out to a cement deck facing the side and back yard. To the side there was a walkway leading around to the front of the house. Off the living room was a small foyer with a stairway leading down to the garage where the cars were kept. The new apartment was finally finished and it was time for her to move in. We were all excited, and Paul and I were ready to share our lives with her.

The day came and for a short time we were one big happy family. We had long nights of talking and getting to know one another. We laughed, and just sat together watching television. Things seemed to be alright.

We always left Bibles and Christian books around the house, which told about our beliefs and faith in Yeshua. One Friday evening we invited her to go to synagogue with us. She felt it was not necessary for her to go and said she was not interested in believing the way we do. We felt that pushing the Bible or God's words on anyone was not the best way to help them, and so we didn't push her. The entire time she was living with us we never pushed or made her feel she was doing anything wrong by not believing the same way we do. I tried with many conversations, but she was not ready to talk.

The first major mistake we made was by not putting a time frame on her stay. Days turned into weeks, weeks turned into months, and months turned into years. When meeting some of our Messianic Jewish friends, she would like some and not others. She couldn't understand how you could believe in Yeshua if you were Jewish, and how some of the Gentiles acted as though they were "trying to be Jews." She wondered why they wanted to be involved in the Jewish holidays, and from what book did we all read? This truly was not her cup of tea.

Things started to shift from good times to trying times. She lost her job and didn't seem concerned about getting another one. There was a sense of disorder in our home and no peace in my heart. I kept thinking what the Bible said:

Lazy hands make a man poor, but diligent hands bring wealth (Proverbs 10:4).

At this point I felt she was lazy and that she didn't care. While she did have some medical problems, I felt she was using them as a crutch. Seeing her staying at home, sitting in a chair, eating and watching TV, reading books all day when both Paul and I were working hard, was not my idea of fun.

There were many excuses of why she did not want to go back to work. She said she tried but there were no jobs in her field. I started to resent this person whom I had really wanted to love. I was not happy to come home after work each day, and weekends became a nightmare. We had so much work that needed to be completed outside the home as well as inside. Paul and I needed help but it was not given. I tried, but no matter what I did, it never seemed to be enough. I came to the place in my heart where it was becoming hardened to her, and no matter what kind of chit-chat she wanted to talk with me, I didn't want to hear anything she had to say. I knew it was time to let go and send her on her way. I found out she was telling my mom we were throwing her out of our home and that we gave her a short time to leave.

Now let me say this about myself: I am not a cream puff. I am not always the good guy, and I can be very stubborn at times. Occasionally I have a bad temper and anger does arise when things do not go well. Things were not going well during this episode and my temper flared more often than not.

I had always felt when I was invited to someone's home for dinner, I would offer to help with the dishes or whatever I could do to show my appreciation to the hostess. If I was invited to stay the night, I would offer to help cook, clean, or just try and be nice. If I was invited to stay at a person's home for an extended amount of time with no rent and free food, I would make sure I did some cooking, cleaned the dishes, cleaned the house, shopped, helped outdoors with the grounds, and anything else I could think of as a way to say thanks for the care that was being shown to me.

God is not a God of disorder but of peace (1 Corinthians 14:33).

I had lost my peace and was growing angrier every day. Paul and I had to admit that our plans did not work out the way we'd hoped they would. Sharon moved back to the state from which she had originally come. I cried the day she left. I had wanted so much for her to enjoy herself and be able to stay here.

As I look back on those years, I realize now that I never asked God to show us *His* will for us in that situation. Should we have taken her in to begin with? I prayed with Paul about it, but I never waited for God's answer or direction. There was no patience on my part to make sure that what I wanted to do was in line with the will of God.

At the time I didn't believe I needed to turn to God to handle anything. I got myself into a huge problem and dealt with it the way I saw fit to bring an end to it. I felt I was the one who needed to be in control of every situation. When I could not work the situation out I became so angry I wanted to explode.

I should not have let issues get so blown out of proportion without discussing them with her. I went to my husband yelling, screaming and wanting him to fix the mess I had made. I should not have complained to others. I needed to look not for approval from man, but to see if God was happy with what I was doing. I needed to be more careful and more considerate of others.

It is now years later and we are many miles apart. Our relationship is not what it was then; in fact, it is better now. We are actually friends. We can talk more and share longer and not have any pressure between us. Of course we are a few years older and we have learned each other's boundaries, and neither one of us has changed in our beliefs. We are both still very Jewish, she in her way, and I as a Jewish believer in Yeshua. We are able to talk with one another about Yeshua in a non-threatening way. We discuss different things we enjoy such as books, television shows, our family, and the Bible.

When I was a brand-new believer I wasn't sure how to handle certain situations or answer many of the difficult questions I was asked. As I continued to read the Bible and mature and grow, I learned more every day of God's wishes and His desires for me to show patience and love for others, even those who are difficult to love. I now try to show others all that He has taught me.

How many times in our lives have we brought family, friends and strangers into our homes because we felt *we* needed and wanted to help them?

How many times have we had bad experiences with different situations in our lives but we still continue doing the same types of things again and again?

How many times does it take for us to stop being stepped on before we learn our lesson?

I cannot answer any of my own questions, because guess what happened to me again? I heard about another person in need and guess what I did?

We Are One

Now is the time to follow Me,
The wicked, oppressed, and lame.
I'll heal the sick, the blind they'll see,
We'll go through the torching flame.

Life goes by on earth so slowly,
With trials, tribulations, and pain.
Don't let My love slip through your spirit,
Remember Me, call out My name.

Why is it so difficult for You to follow Me?
I offer peace and everlasting life.
Remove your veils and blinders to see,
I'm your bridegroom, you are My wife.

You are My children; I'll never leave you alone,
Walk with Me, talk to Me, cry out your pain.
At the end of them when all is done,
I am one, the Father, Holy Spirit, and Son.

Merle Debra

Chapter 11

Why Did I Do It Again?

One would think if you tried something you felt was a good idea and the results did not turn out for the best, or if feelings were hurt and we didn't see God's love through the ordeal, you would not do it a second time. Guess again. I fell victim to a bleeding heart's cry for the second time. In both instances I did pray about the situation, and I believed it was the right thing to do. Oh, my goodness, was I wrong.

I received a phone call from a friend asking me to pray for a friend of hers who was in need of help. As Hattie returned home from work, she turned the corner to go into her apartment complex. As she got closer she noticed her belongings were on the street. The apartment complex manager had evicted her from her apartment while she was at work during the day. As she tried to get all her things in her car she realized the larger electronic items were gone. Missing was her brand new vacuum, VCR, radio, television, and some other small items. The only things that were left were her clothes, kitchen and bathroom articles, a few cans of food, a few tables, and a couch. I was asked to pray she would find a place to live until she could save some money and get another apartment. Here we go again.

By this time Paul had moved his office back downstairs. He was comfortable and very happy to have his large room back again. I knew I could not ask him to move upstairs again. In my heart I felt like we should do something because we had an extra bedroom upstairs near ours that she could use. I was told she had a job and would only be in our home for a short time until she could get herself back on her feet again. I mentioned I may be able to house her but that I needed to speak with Paul before making a decision.

Once again, after giving Paul another hard-luck story, he told me if I felt this was the right thing to do then to just go ahead. You have to understand, Paul has a heart that is so big and so gentle. He would never turn anyone away. He brings in strays of any kind. Paul would feed anyone and give money to anyone who would cry. He is Mister Softy to the bone. Of course he said yes, but he also told me to really think hard about it this time. He travels most of the time for his job, and I would be the one with her all the time. I felt alright with the situation. I called my friend back and told her how Paul and I would be willing to have her move in with us. Hattie needed to call and set up a time to come and see where we lived to determine if it was too far from work and if the bedroom would be large enough for all her clothing.

Needless to say, she was impressed and in love with our home and said she would feel comfortable living with us. She said she would start moving in two days. Hattie was going to be staying with another friend only for a couple of days and on the weekend would move in with us. I had only two days to get the room ready and empty the closet where I stored our extra clothes. We have two full bathrooms upstairs. One is off of our bedroom, and the other is the guest bathroom. I emptied the two side drawers and the entire cabinet on the bottom. We were more than happy to give her full run of the house and to have her help herself with all the food in the cabinets and in the freezer. I made space in the kitchen cabinets for the food she had brought, and then had cable TV installed in her room.

Once again I made my biggest mistake: I did not give her a timeframe. Now I was beginning to tread in dirty waters. I did not tell Hattie what I expected from her, and when things went wrong I let them slip by again.

At the time she was living with us I was not working and so I was able to cook and have hot meals ready for her when she came home from work. The nights Paul was out of town the table would be set, the food was kept warm, and I waited to eat until she came home from work so she would have someone to eat dinner with and not be alone. She was grateful for two weeks. The nights she came home late I would still have her dinner ready. She never had to use any of her own food. In fact, when she left she still had the same food in the cabinet that she brought with her the first day. We had some good days where we would talk and get to know one another a little better. We talked about our children, marriages, and had many deep and loving conversations. Our Yeshua was discussed at every chance we had, and we prayed together once in a while. Every morning at five o'clock she would get on the phone with her prayer partners and pray until seven when she had to leave for work. I believe that was a saving grace time for her. She would tell me how great it had been and how blessed she felt whenever she got off the phone. Unfortunately, I was never invited to listen in or be part of her phone group.

One day I was sick and Hattie was a little late coming home from work. She came into the house and asked what was for dinner. I told her I was sick with a bad cold and did not prepare dinner. She said she was sorry that I felt bad, but again she asked, "So what are we having for dinner?" I had heated up some soup and offered her what was left. She went upstairs to change and came down when she was ready.

*A hot-tempered man stirs up dissension, but
a patient man calms a quarrel
(Proverbs 15:18).*

One evening I knocked on her door to ask her a question and she was eating some food on her bed. I asked her to please not bring food into her room and that I would appreciate it if she would eat it in the kitchen because I didn't want to get bugs in the house. The next day there she was, still eating in her room, and now there were bags of chips, nuts, cookies, and candy. Did she do it out of spitefulness or what?

Whoever loves discipline love knowledge, but he who hates discipline is stupid (Proverbs 2:1).

By this time I was really starting to lose my temper. I called friends asking for prayer for patience. Now I had to tell Paul, my loving husband, that I had done it again. I was getting frustrated. I couldn't pray. I couldn't talk to God. I couldn't hear direction from God, and my patience was running so very thin. I thought everyone expressed gratitude in a certain way, with good, decent behavior, and with thoughtfulness and a conscience. The questions rolled around in my mind constantly. *Where did I go wrong? What did I ever do to deserve this? God, where are you?* With maturity I would eventually learn that He had been there all along, but I had not really been listening.

Paul said there was an easy solution: just ask her to leave.

Hattie had a bad knee and had to have surgery. I helped her in any way I could. I brought her back from the hospital after surgery. We have two flights of stairs and she was not allowed to walk up and down; the doctors wanted her to stay on one level. I cooked the foods she liked, helped give her the right medicines, and made her as comfortable as possible.

Then it happened. She lost her job.

I can't go through this again, I thought wearily.

After her recovery I was leaving to attend a weekend conference in Florida with a friend. I explained to Hattie this would be a perfect time for her to consider looking for her own place. It would be best for all of us, especially for my husband, if she was not left alone with him for four days. I told her this almost two months in advance. I wanted her to know I was not just throwing her out with no notice, even though to her it may have felt like I was.

From the very beginning I expressed to Hattie how much I loved my dogs and that she needed to be very careful to keep the gates shut in the backyard. If any of them were left open and the dogs saw them opened they would charge right out and get lost. The day came when she was ready to leave. She made many trips back and forth to the car with her boxes. I was not with her when she made her last trip.

Earlier that day I had let the dogs out to play. Later I asked Paul if he had seen the dogs? He hadn't seen them for a short time. We went out to the side of the house and he noticed she had left the gate open. My dogs were out and they were running. Paul and I ran out to the street where I saw Shana. I called to her and started running to her. Thank God she came running back. Samantha, at the time, was a young two-year-old who thought this newfound freedom was great, and she kept running. Our neighbors were just starting to drive out of their driveway. I called to them and asked them to please drive down the street to see if Samantha would get in the car with them so they could bring her back. She knew them and would go in the car if they could catch her. They drove all over the neighborhood trying to find her. A few times she saw them but was quicker and just kept running. A gentleman I never knew was driving down the street and heard us calling for her. He had seen her up the street and told me to get in the car and he would drive me to where he last saw her. We spotted her, so I jumped out of the car and called her several times but she kept running. At this point she was scared and not sure who any of us were. I called our ex-guest and told her the dogs had gotten loose because she had left the gate door open. She was not too bothered by it. I yelled as loud as I could and asked her if she was coming back to help us catch the dogs.

A gentle answer turns away wrath, but a harsh word stirs up anger (Proverbs 15:1).

I know that wasn't the best thing to do, but I was so angry. My anger got the best of me. Because of my yelling and screaming, I guess she got the hint. She showed up some time later to try and help, but she couldn't catch the dog so she just left. I didn't want to feel she had done it out of spite. I prayed it was just her forgetfulness, but at that time I believed she wanted to get even with me.

Finally Samantha did come home, and Paul was waiting in the yard for her. She was so tired, nervous, and just wanted to be loved. When he brought her into the house, all I could do was cry. Lord, Hattie had sure tested my patience, which was totally gone by this time. What did I learn from this mess? Never to do it again!

How many of us have thought we were doing something good to help God out? How many of us would do it again and again, never learning what it was we were supposed to learn from the first time? We are not to stop helping others, but we are to use wisdom in all circumstances. God is a God of second chances. We should not let the sun go down while we're still angry at someone. When we do anything, we should do it for God and not man.

When you are mad, discuss it with the other person. Do not let it eat you up, because eventually it might be too late. Sometimes things are not apparent to both parties at the same time. People can't read your mind. Man can let you down, but God is always for you. Sometimes there may be consequences if we are not listening to God's direction. And last but not least, we are to love one another and realize that friendship is better than all the diamonds, gold, and treasures of the world.

Will I do this again?

If I do, I will make sure it is done God's way, in God's timing, and with God's blessings.

Father's Day

For My Dad

To be with you on Father's Day,
Is more than I can ask for.
Your love, laughter, and the crazy things you say,
Who could ask for anything more.

My love for you is deep within,
My heart is always yours.
To go against you would be the greatest sin,
I'd feel like a bird that never soars.

Thanks for being my special dad,
In good and troubled times.
Just think of all the happy times we've had,
And this poem, and how it rhymes.

Merle Debra

Chapter 12

There's No Such Thing As a Little White Lie

Have you ever loved someone so much you would be willing to excuse their behavior?

I was known in my family as my daddy's princess. My sister, who is three years older, reminded me daily, saying, "You're Daddy's favorite; he loves you more than us; you're his princess." I knew it was true and I loved every minute of it. Then and now, I would never deny it. It never seemed to bother my brother who was three years younger, maybe because he was a boy and didn't feel the comparison like my sister did. Whatever my mom felt, she never let it show. Unfortunately, though, my royal status did not help me when I got myself into a lot of trouble.

My father was not a scholar, but he had a very vivid imagination. He was a fabulous story teller about any person, place, or thing. His stories were so real, and the way he told them made you think for sure that no one could possibly make up a story like that. He came up with strange names, dates, places; imaginary people with first, middle, and last names from every country in the world, all of which sounded true. His stories were picturesque. My dad seemed to get away with any story if anyone would listen. Dad was always the life of a party and a stand-up comedian. He really should have been on the stage. He loved people, but not his life. Dad saw his father only one time in his life when he was thirteen. His mother had remarried and didn't want her son (my dad) living with her and her new husband. He was sent to live with his aunt and uncle and their five daughters, who lived not far from his mom. Work was necessary if he wanted to continue living with them. He was told that he would have to give part of his pay to his aunt. My dad was a handsome man who could knock you over with his smile and great looks. His mother had always dressed him with the finest suits possible before sending him away. She loved to make sure he always looked prim and proper.

My dad did not enjoy school, but once he got out he worked well in the retail business, feeding and taking care of his family and his other loves: smoking cigarettes, drinking, and gambling, along with other bad habits.

One afternoon while we were still living at home, the phone rang. My brother, who was reaching his teen years, picked up the phone and said hello. The man on the other end of the phone said if our father did not pay up or stop fooling around we would find him dead. My brother hung up the phone quickly.

He was white as a ghost and scared to death. After that call, many times when the phone would ring my brother wouldn't answer it, even if he was standing right next to it. Unfortunately, there was a dark side to this funny, loving man I knew as my father.

When we were younger and living in New Jersey, my dad worked in a hardware store, which belonged to my mother's family. The store was located in the next town, South Amboy. The store also sold children's toys, and dad was always bringing home games and toys for us. He would bring home dolls, doll houses, and bassinets. My brother got the bats, balls and gloves. I tried to tell dad I also wanted the balls, bats and gloves. It was my sister who loved the dolls. I loved climbing trees, playing ball, and getting in the mud.

The business went through its ups and downs. The store was hit by a hurricane. Just before the store was hit, my dad and all the men ran out. They were so afraid. They had absolutely no idea where they were going. They knew they just needed to run. The store was rebuilt the first time it was destroyed.

A second disaster occurred when was a bomb exploded in the river. Again the store was hit, and rebuilt.

The third and final time, a fire entirely destroyed the building. This time the family was not willing to rebuild it again. Since it was not my dad's store, he had to accept the decisions made by others. Everyone working there had to find other jobs, including my dad.

Dad and I could always sit and talk about anything. No matter how angry my dad became with me, there was never a time he didn't want to at least sit with me. Sometimes we would just silent together. When I was young dad would pick me up and put my feet on the tops of his feet and dance with me. He twirled me around the room and we would laugh together. Whenever I cried about something he made me laugh with some of his jokes. I had heard some of them over and over, but it didn't matter because he was my dad and I loved him.

My mother, on the other hand, had rough times with him constantly. He would come home drunk, but I never saw or heard him hit or abuse any of us. One night when my dad came home drunk he got undressed and went to jump into bed, only he missed the bed and ended up on the floor. My mom got up, put a blanket on him and left him there. When they told us about it the next day, I thought it was hysterical. I always thought my dad was funny when he was drunk. I'm sure my mom didn't appreciate any of the things dad did when he was drunk whether they were meant to be funny or not.

One time our family went to a party at a country club with a lot of our parents' friends and their children. At the end of the evening my dad took his keys off the hook of the valet parking pad, put them in his pocket, and then he took all the other keys on the pad, mixed them up, and threw them in a pile. No one could find their keys for hours. The phone rang all night until everyone found their keys and could finally go home.

I never realized how hard it was for my mom. She never said anything bad about him. Mom worked hard at home making sure all the meals were cooked and the house was cleaned. She took care of the family's needs. She shopped wisely and was smart with handling the finances. She never complained to us. We were always in bed and asleep early so when my dad came home they had their time together.

There were a few times when I was older, that my friends and I went to the neighborhood bar. I would find my dad drunk. I would take him home then go back out with my friends to drink. Unfortunately I acquired some of my dad's nasty habits. My dad made me cover for him by either buying him out of trouble, rescuing him when he became involved with someone he should not have been involved with, and a few times, wanted me to lie for him. I have asked my mom why she and Dad didn't get a divorce. Her answer: There was no place for her to go with three children. Dad had no money, and so where was he to go? I believe my parents loved each other but negative things always seemed to get in the way. Watching my parents in later years, I realized my dad really did love my mother and was truly sorry for the things he had put her through. Some things are easy to forgive. It's the forgetting part that is hard.

On one of the many occasions when Dad had been gone for days and we had no idea where he was, Mom hired a private investigator to find out if he indeed was still alive. He was in a place he should not have been.

Dad had been involved with another woman and had been living with her and her family. He lied about his marriage but not about his children. We were all grown and married and lived in different areas by then. He tried to end the relationship and she ended up calling me. I was pregnant at the time, and her call upset me. Paul was concerned and tried to calm me down. Dad promised her the world, but when she found out he was married she told me she was going to call my mother. I told her never to contact my mother. I told her that Dad would never marry her and that he still truly loved my mom and was going back to live with her. I suggested she step out of the way and stay out of my mother's life. I told her I was sorry for all the things that had happened. I asked her to never contact any one of us again. Now there were two families involved in being hurt. She did vanish from our lives, probably in pain from the hurt and lies. Dad was very smart and a good liar. He never lied to me, but sometimes I wished I had not been part of his plans. I wish I hadn't hurt my mother so much by being a part of his schemes.

Recently I went to my mother and asked for her forgiveness. For many years I had felt something has not been right between us, and sure enough there was something she had carried around in her heart for at least thirty-four years. She was upset that I had lied to her about the other woman. All those years ago I didn't want my mom to find out and be hurt, so I thought it would be better not to tell her. I was trying to protect her. In this case, I was so very wrong and caused her more harm. For years Mom had a problem with my father, his lies, and with me not telling her the truth when she needed to hear it, no matter what the stories were. I was so sorry for the pain I had caused her. I had never intended to hurt her or take sides.

I have just recently come to an understanding in my own heart that a child is not responsible for his or her parents' actions. A child is not supposed to take sides with one parent. A child should not be made to lie or cover up things that are wrong between adults, or to hurt one parent by smoothing things out for the other parent. The parents are in charge of the children, not the other way around. My dad always told me it was my job to take care of my mother and do right by her, but it seemed as though it was alright for him to do whatever he pleased. I wanted to love my mom simply because I loved her, not because I *had* to love her.

It is not easy being a child trying to help a parent keep lies from the rest of the family, nor is it easy being the parent telling little white lies to keep the family from being hurt. Either way, no one wins. God is a God of truth and love. Without God in our lives we do not feel convicted in our hearts. We are often told as children that if we only tell a little white lie then there's no harm in it. The only problem is, a lie is a lie, no matter how small or how big. It is wrong and it will hurt someone eventually.

Dad was a hugger and a kisser. Whenever he would see my brother he always had a hug and a kiss for him. That sensitivity and love was passed on to my husband. My dad was a loving, caring man, and he learned many harsh lessons in his life, and many times had asked the good Lord for forgiveness. I have never wished for a different childhood or adulthood, or wished for any other kind of parent for one second, no matter what we went through. All in all, we are a very close family. We would do anything for any one of us at any given time.

Peace of Mind

My Dad's Birthday

You are my dad,
And I love you so.
Never to question,
Always you'll know.

Our hearts are bonded,
As one thick rope.
If ever to loosen,
We always have hope.

We've shared our hopes, dreams, and past,
Never misjudging each other.
Our silent moments soon will come,
But God will bless you to be with your mother.

Each year you're with me, I treasure our moments,
Our walks, talks, and peaceful sunsets.
We laugh, we cry, we hug and sit silent,
Hold hands, just smile, never a need to be violent.

We'll be all right, and time will go on,
You'll always be in my heart.
We have that special unbreakable bond,
I love you, Dad, you'll "NEVER BE GONE."

Merle Debra
May 9

Chapter 13

Every Second Counts

We were a close family until the day I decided to accept Yeshua.

When I became a completed Jew, a Messianic Jew, a Jewish believer, my parents would not hear of it. My mother would say, "Don't ever talk about it in front of your father; it would devastate him." My father would say, "Don't talk about it in front of your mother; it would kill her."

In 1992 I gave my parents a book titled, *The Living Scriptures*, hoping they would at least read the words I wrote to them on the inside of the cover:

Mom and Dad,

He has made His wonders to be remembered;

The Lord is gracious and compassionate
— Psalm 111:4.

The fear of the Lord is the beginning of wisdom;

A good understanding have all those who do His commandment.

His praise endures forever — Psalm 111:10

Because we love you, we give you this Bible

Forever our love,
Paul and Merle

Mom and Dad came to visit, but they did not stay as long as usual. Before they left, Mom handed me the book I'd given them with a note inside for me:

Merle - This book has brought evil into our house, our home. It has twisted your mind, lost our love and friendship. Because we won't follow you, you have ignored us completely. **Two very hurt, very sad, very sick and very lonely parents** *(in bold letters)*

Since that evening our years together have been hard. At the beginning they were just putting up with me, now it is more harmful. My mom would keep asking me, as she still does, "Merle, why have you converted from being a Jew?" She still feels I am no longer Jewish; I am now one of "them." She said my decision was killing both of them. I would be an embarrassment to her and her friends if ever they found out. She can't bear for me to speak the name "Jesus." When I want to talk about her questions she tells me she doesn't want to hear and then gets very angry. Many evenings I have cried myself to sleep not wanting to hurt my parents, but I cannot deny the fact I am a Jewish believer in Yeshua.

Every summer, for many years, our entire family would go together on vacations to the beach. After a few years of becoming a follower of Yeshua, my parents told me they weren't sure if they would go with us on any more vacations, because we would read "that" book and listen to "that" music. They were uncomfortable with all of the things we were now doing. Our times spent together were different now and they didn't appreciate that.

Fathers, do not exasperate your children (Ephesians 6:4).

A few years later when my parents would come over to visit, my dad would sometimes pick up some of the different books I had purposely left on the end tables in the living room. If no one was watching he would read some portions of them. When he thought someone was coming into the room he would put the book back down. When I saw him pick one up I would stay out of the room on purpose to give him time to read. My father told me he knew a Jewish priest who would come into the bar where he went many nights in New Jersey. He would discuss the Bible with him. He knows something about Jesus.

I tried to have some conversations about the Bible with my parents. Mom would always look up, sigh, and want to finish the conversation. I believe Dad, on the other hand, wanted to talk more. One question Dad always had was why there were so many interpretations of the Bible. He believes there is only one book, one way, with the same words. He believed man changed the writings to fit their own beliefs, which were different from the Jewish book. Why would they need so many different interpretations?

When my dad was seventy-six, he promised his granddaughter and great-grandchildren he would take them to Disney World in Florida. The trip would take us thirteen hours of driving. My dad was a man of his word. He was not feeling well and had to take an oxygen tank for his emphysema. Mom and Dad and Paul and I drove down in one car. Stacy, our daughter, Greg, our son- in-law and our three grandchildren — Stephanie, Shelby Rhea, and Gregory — drove down in their car.

Dad played with the kids as much as he could. We rented a wheelchair for Dad to help him get around easier. None of us realized how much pain he was suffering. He stayed in the hotel much of the time, saying he was just very tired. I wish I had been more observant to see how much pain he was suffering. He loved his family and would do anything for any one of us. I do not think he knew it was the bitter end either.

My dad loved his granddaughter and his great-grandchildren. He read them stories, played games, and even made up some of his wildest children's stories. They would all laugh, have a wonderful time, and smother each other with kisses.

The last night of our vacation we all went out to eat in the hotel restaurant. Dad was so sick he wanted to go back to his room and go to bed. I told mom to stay with the family and I would take him back. I helped him into the bed. While he was sitting against his pillow I held his hand, and as I looked into his eyes he started to cry. I heard him say something about how he wanted to go home. I told him we would be leaving in the morning. Dad said "No, I want to go home," meaning to be with God.

I leaned closer and looked deeply into his eyes and started to cry. I told him I was not ready for him to leave me yet. I guess I didn't know how sick he really was. I wiped my eyes when the family started to come in. I couldn't bear to tell them what he had said. We all went to sleep early. The next day we would be heading home, and it would be another long drive.

The ride home must have been an awful experience for my dad. He was in so much pain. As we were driving, I don't remember what happened, but my dad and I had a disagreement and spoke some harsh words to one another. We made a stop for everybody to take a bathroom break and get some snacks, but when my dad had to get out of the car to go into the bathroom, he looked so bent over, his hair seemed so white, and he looked so sad. Paul had to help Dad walk, he was so weak. I felt so awful that I had argued with him in this frail condition. When we all got back into the car, I apologized and asked for his forgiveness. He smiled his crooked smile and told me he loved me, and I told him I loved him also. The way home was not bad from then on.

*Honor your mother and father
(Deuteronomy 5:16).*

Greg helped me take my parents up to their apartment. We kissed them and returned to each of our homes.

In the morning my mom called and told me she had to take my dad to the hospital. From my home they live only a half-hour away. When I got to the hospital, I went into the emergency room where my dad was being cared for. He looked so sick, so pasty white in color, so frail. We were waiting for test results to be completed. The doctor told us Dad was in kidney failure and needed more tests. The tests were painful for my dad and he started to cry. He couldn't go through anymore of the tests. We were told they had seen what they needed to see, and he could go back to his room. The medical technician came over to me and told me he was so sorry, but there was nothing left to do. Dad's body was completely eaten up with cancer.

The doctor told us he was so sorry; he explained that Dad had twenty-four hours left to live at the most. Most of his organs had shut down, and the rest would not take long to shut down also. We were all in shock. I wanted to pass out. My mom's face was indescribable. Dad was admitted to the hospital for what would be his last hours.

My husband, God bless him, went home and made reservations to have my sister and brother flown to Georgia within hours. We were all allowed to sleep in his room for the remainder of his time with us here on earth. There are no words to describe that evening. How do you try to explain the deep pain and nervousness you go through? When you sit with your dad for his final moments of life, you realize you will not be leaving the hospital and bringing him back home with you. You realize you will never get to see him again, never hear his laughter, or even hear him yelling and screaming for whatever reason. I wasn't ready to let him go. I needed him. Next to my husband he was my best friend in the world. I truly loved my dad and wasn't ready for him to leave.

My dad slipped in and out of a semi-coma, awakening with cries of pain. The doctor asked what he could do to help keep him comfortable in his remaining hours, and I told him to please not let him be in any pain. They ordered morphine shots every two hours. The pulmonary team brought in a machine for me to use to help with the mucus that would need to be drained out of his mouth to keep him from drowning in his saliva. I wanted my dad to not have a painful death. After all, he was my dad. He was, little by little, slipping away from me. A strong man who used to hold me, laugh with me, and even fight with me because of our bad tempers, was leaving me forever.

Dad and I would take long walks on the beach. When we would vacation together we would sit on our chairs in the water, just staring at the waves. We could sit there for hours, never needing to speak, just holding hands and being in peace. He had the softest hands for a man of not large statue. He was my dad, and I couldn't believe he would soon be gone.

My parent's apartment was next door to the hospital. My sister, brother, and mom went to my mom's house to shower and get something to eat. My dad had just received a shot and was sleeping with such a peaceful look on his face. I needed some peace as well. I took my Bible and read Psalm 23 out loud to my dad, and I anointed him with oil and prayed for him. I would not leave my dad for one second. I held his hand in mine, stroked his frail fingers, ran my hand through his messed up hair, kissed his soft face, and cried tears on his chest. *Dad, don't leave me yet.*

After a little while my family returned and we all sat and just stared at one another. We couldn't believe what was happening. I was so thankful we were together. Mom went into the bathroom, and came out when she heard us all walk around to the bed. We gathered around my dad when all of a sudden he gasped a deep breath and stopped breathing. A few seconds later he started to breathe again. I knew his next breath would be his last. During the last seconds of my dad's life, he sat up in his bed and looked straight at me. My sister said, "Oh, my God, look at his face." His color had changed; his face was radiant, his eyes were fully opened and clear, he smiled, and then he laid back down on his pillow and drew his last breath.

God was so gracious to let me be with my dad in the last seconds of his life. I was able to see the peace come upon his face after being in so much pain. Standing in front of my dad watching his last second of life, I knew in my heart Yeshua had come and showed Himself to my dad. I believe my dad said "yes" to Yeshua. I imagined him walking hand in hand together with Yeshua as He welcomed Dad to his heavenly home. I had been praying for nine years, and my heart's desire was for Dad to except Yeshua. I believe in the last second of his life it happened. The rest of my family did not understand what I believed had just taken place.

My earthly father is now in the loving arms of my heavenly Father. I can't wait until I'll be able to hold both of their hands. I will thank them for loving me just as I am.

Dad On His Deathbed

As I sit with you by your bedside,
Wondering what is going through your mind.
God knows my deep love I have for you.
But sometimes you're so hard to find.

You're nervous, scared, and bewildered
Not knowing the right thing to do.
Keep trying and stay alive, or to let go
Is the choice that is left up to you.

There are so many things God has for you,
It's never too late to be shown.
Keep trying to fight for your family,
There are children that haven't even grown.

You have so much to offer them,
Your stories, attention, and love.
Your time isn't now to give up
You can't kiss and hug them from above.

Stand firm; don't let yourself give up
We're here to help you walk slow.
You can make life worthwhile,
When time is over God will come, you'll see Him glow.

Merle Debra
June 22, 1998

Mom

As you sit by his bedside in the hospital,
Not knowing just what to expect.
You have followed your heart to help him,
With caring love, you've seen great effects.

Sometimes pride overtakes a body,
Because of who they wanted to become.
It doesn't seen fair to the other half,
It's insensitive and not caring to some.

You have always been a caring mother,
A loving and faithful wife.
Your laughter and your beautiful smile,
A friend with no anger or strife.

My greatest prayer for you is peace,
God's love, always showering over you.
My love for you my dear mother,
Your decisions, or whatever you do.

I have never taken you for granted,
Never meant to ever cause you pain.
We're always here for each other,
With a deeper love, only to gain.

Merle Debra
June 22, 1998

My Daughter, Stacy Rhea

My daughter I treasure our moments,
Beating jointly we've become one heart.
God gave you to me with His blessings,
Which I thank Him, each day we're apart.

Your smile to all is with radiance,
Your laughter brings joy to all.
Your beauty comes from deep within you,
Your love that you share breaks down walls.

I pray that God's mercy will follow you,
All the days you are here on His earth.
For your goodness and loving compassion,
Is all God has taught us since birth.

He has given you two daughters to cherish,
To watch them grown up with your love.
They are as special to you as you are to me,
A love unblemished, as a pure white dove.

My daughter, I love you for always,
I'm proud of who you have become.
You're my gift from God, whom I treasure forever.
From now till the end of your days.

Stand tall, and never be worried,
I'll always be here for you.
Though happy or sad, sickness or health,
I'll stand by you, whatever you do.

I'm A Jew I Don't Do Jesus

I will always love you, Stacy Rhea,
Wherever you may go.
My heart will always be with you,
No matter where the winds may blow.

Merle Debra
June 22, 1998

Chapter 14

Mexico, Ready or Not, Here I Come

I n August of 2006 the Lord led me to two wonderful Christian friends, a woman named Virginia and her husband Jerry. One day I called Virginia and asked her if she would like to meet me for lunch and she kindly accepted. We met at a restaurant halfway between our homes. We talked about our friends, our grandchildren, our kids, and shared about her past missionary trips. I have always wanted to do missions work, but the opportunity never seemed to come along at the right time. A few of my friends had traveled to Africa but I never felt led to go. Truthfully, I do believe one reason I have never wanted to go to Africa, is because I am afraid of all the many different types of shots I would have to get. I am a baby when it comes to getting shots and taking large amounts of medicine, and the chances of getting sick or having a bad reaction from any shots seemed to great to risk it. I have had my share of sicknesses, and adding one more was not on my list of things I wanted to accomplish in life.

Virginia's son was having lunch with some other missionaries at a different table close by. After he finished his lunch he and the other men came over to our table to say hello. He introduced himself and told me a little about his missionary ministry. I was so impressed and excited I felt a pounding in my heart. The ministry he heads visits three different countries, Mexico, Africa, and the Dominican Republic. The men with him were from Africa. They were meeting to discuss the food they were trying to get to the people, and the trip he was planning to make to Africa soon. Her son mentioned about how one team would be going to Mexico in the next three months. He asked if I wanted to go with the team and stated there was only one spot left on the list. The mission team could only have seventeen people go at one time. Two vans would be driving and only seven or eight people could ride in each van. At that time there were sixteen signed up, with a waiting list of five people. I was told there were no real shot requirements, only a passport which I had already acquired. Virginia told me she and Jerry were going on this mission trip and felt it would be a wonderful experience for me. They had been to Mexico a few times in the past and explained to me what it might be like. At that moment I was asked, do you want to go? Jerry was in charge of some of the arrangements for the group, and if I wanted to go, I had two seconds left to make up my mind. Without hesitation, out of my mouth came, yes, I want on the list, I want to go to Mexico. Virginia reached for her cell phone and saw on the screen that her husband Jerry had tried to call us several times during lunch but she never heard the phone ring. She dialed Jerry and when she finally got ahold of him we told him I wanted to go on the mission trip and for him to call to put my name on the list. Later I was told there was one opening left when he called, and so now my name was officially on the team list. We finished our lunch and as we were walking out it hit me full force: I would be going to Mexico on a mission tent project in three months! I knew in my heart it was the right thing to do. I became so excited I couldn't wait to tell Paul.

The team met for the first time on a Sunday in a trailer next to the main church building. Getting to the building early I saw a gentleman waiting in his car. I went over to him, introduced myself, and asked if he was attending the meeting for the mission trip. He said he was but wasn't sure if he should be going. The pastor from the church he attended was going, and both he and his wife thought it would be good support for their pastor. He was having second thoughts, however. We talked for a few minutes and I gave him some encouragement, and when the others showed up we both happily went into the trailer knowing he was called to go.

It was so exciting to meet the others who had also decided to go on this trip. We numbered eight women and nine men. There was an equal amount of us who had never been on a mission trip before. The meeting came to order led by our team leader, Randy, and

Jerry, his assistant. First there was prayer and meditation time. Next we all introduced ourselves and told whatever we felt would help others get to know us better. The pros and cons of being in Mexico were explained to the group, such as the weather, what our team was going to be doing in Mexico, conditions of the homes, and what our schedule would be like. Of course the schedule was subject to change once we were there depending on the weather and so forth.

There would be a large tent put up in an area where no other missionaries had been before. We would be feeding the people of this area, a doctor would be with us to give free medical care, a mobile pharmacy would provide medicine, and a dentist would be there to fill cavities and extract teeth as needed. There would be prayer available in another tent off to the side. In the evenings we would be having music, testimonies, a message from the pastor, worshipful dance, and many activities for the children. My heart was pounding once again with excitement as I heard about all the things we would be experiencing.

There were, of course, a few forms we needed to fill out and we were told we only needed to have a passport. Since I hadn't had any shots in a long time I chose to get a tetanus and hepatitis shot. Not knowing what I might get myself into, I felt it would be a smart move on my part to do so. After getting the shots, one in each arm at the same time, I had flu-like symptoms for two days and had to rest and take it easy. I had dreaded this, but thankfully I felt better within a few days.

Driving from Georgia to Mexico would take about twenty-six hours. In the van we were all allowed to take our blankets, pillows, and whatever snacks or drinks we would need. I have a favorite pillow and blanket I take whenever I go on trips in the car and was glad I could take them. We were told to take clothes for warm days as well as cold rainy ones, and hats to protect our heads from the sun. If we were to bring a camera it needed to be in our possession at all times. I decided to bring my little PHD ("push here, dummy") camera instead of my expensive one. I was afraid I might put it down and leave it somewhere in all the busyness and excitement.

Our group met every Sunday afternoon for three weeks to prepare for the trip. We were given room assignments, and I was so excited to learn that my friend Virginia would be rooming with me. After the meeting the real questions came out. Do you snore, do you go to bed late, do you take morning or evening showers? I do not know why women get so concerned with these things. The men are more down-to-earth: they find their roommate, go into their room, undress, get into bed, and go to sleep, not caring about anything. We women can be so complicated.

At one of the Sunday meetings, each of us signed up to lead a daily devotional meeting once we were in Mexico: we could offer a prayer, read a story, share a testimony of ourselves or someone we had come in contact with while in Mexico. These devotionals were to be led in the morning before going out for the day's mission work and in the evening before dinner and our nighttime service. I signed up for a morning time slot and decided that whatever Yeshua gave to me while I was there would be my devotional.

The two vans left on a Friday morning, while six of us would be flying out on Saturday morning, meeting the van in Texas. After arriving in Texas, the flyers still had a nine- to ten-hour drive to get to our final destination in Mexico. We stopped for lunch at a barbeque restaurant, which was our leader's favorite place, then headed out to a hotel in Laredo, Texas for the first night.

Our cook and our dentist would be flying into Mexico the first day of the tent project. That was the earliest they could get away from their regular jobs.

On our first evening together we checked into our rooms, and then we all met in one of the meeting rooms for prayer and our first devotion time together. This was a special time of really getting to know our hearts' desires. We prayed for each person in the room for whatever they felt they needed prayer for. A song was played for meditation time with words of praise to the Lord, thanking Him for travel mercies for the day and for others still to come. Prayers were lifted up to our God for the next day when we had to go to the borders to have our paperwork signed. We prayed there would be no problems, no sickness, and that the Mexican police would find favor with us to let us through quickly. Prayer was a major part of our daily lives, especially when we were in the hands of others in another country or state. We knew nothing was impossible with God.

Early the next morning we all met in the meeting room for our devotional, prayers, and a quick breakfast. Our mission was to get our papers signed, passports stamped, vans and trailers registered, and then to get out as fast as possible to begin the work we'd come there to do. We prayed continually. The volunteers who'd been on mission trips before said all of this work could take anywhere from one hour to all day to get done. We seemed to have arrived at the Mexican permit station at a good time, because no one else was in line. In a short amount of time we received our papers and were allowed to move on. Now the heavy-hitting prayers were needed. Both vans still had two checkpoints to go through. Those could take anywhere from two to ten hours. If they chose to do so, the Mexican police could make us unload everything out of the vans to allow them to check the contents, and then we would have to pack them up again. They could choose to take anything they felt we did not need to take with us. God showed us tremendous favor. The police opened only one of the vans and they had us move a few things from one van to another for safety reasons. We were on our way within an hour. Isn't God good when He is on your side?!

One checkpoint down, one more to go. As we approached the second one, there were numerous police and army men all around on both sides of the road carrying rifles and machetes. We heard that usually nothing got by any of these men without a thorough and time-consuming search. Once again God showed us favor and our vans were both waved through. As we all held our breath, still praying, our two vans drove slowly through the checkpoint. Thank you, Lord!

Finally we reached our destination of Monterrey, Mexico. We had been invited to church services with the pastor, who would also be helping us set up, and we met the people in the area where our tent project was to be held. The church delayed their services until we arrived. During the service we joined in as much as we could with the singing. Through the services of preaching God's Word and scripture readings, the congregation made us feel right at home. As we shook hands they gave us hugs, welcomed us all to their country, and already were thanking us for being part of their lives. We were beginning to feel a part of their family, even with our language barrier. I spoke no Spanish, and they spoke no English, but I felt so attached to them already.

We were introduced to the women and men who would be helping us with prayer in the prayer tents and the men who would be singing and playing the music during the evening sessions. Approximately seven to ten blocks away was where the tents were being set up on a large, square dirt area surrounded by the homes of the people.

I cried from the minute we drove into the area until we left to go back to the hotel. My heart couldn't handle the sadness I was feeling. The children were running in the streets. Some of them were without shoes and wandering around by themselves

The animals in the neighborhood were pitiful; you could see every bone in their body sticking out.

They walked with their backs hunched over, and their heads bent low. There was one small dog the size of a miniature poodle that scratched its body on the cement for so long there was no hair, only the pink skin. This dog had to stay underneath cars because the sun was so strong, and because its skin was so pink the sun was painful to him. I am a true lover of animals, and I couldn't bear to look at any of the dogs. We were told never to touch or pick them up because they had not had shots and probably were infested with ticks and fleas.

A few of the children came running over to us when they saw the tent going up. There was so much excitement among them and they started talking so fast in Spanish, I didn't know what they were saying, but I knew it had to be good. One of the gentlemen on our team was a translator in three languages. Everywhere I went, whenever someone wanted to talk to me, I yelled for him frantically, saying, "Where are you?! Help, what do they want? What are they saying?!" Most of the team kept calling for him all week for help with translation, and I was so thankful he was with us. We explained to the children we would be back in a few hours to start our evening music and preaching. We told them to go and get all their friends and family, and we would meet them in a few hours. In groups of twos and threes our team handed out flyers to the people in the surrounding area. Lights were strung, the tent was completed, ropes were tied down, the stage was built where the music and preaching was to be held, and soon we were ready for action.

From the minute we arrived a young boy of around eleven rushed over to me, put his arm around my waist, and wouldn't let go. He had a smile that could light up the world. On the back of his head were a few strands of hair standing straight up like Dennis the Menace. Needless to say, I fell in love with him. The team was warned not to leave the area with anyone alone, and to make sure at least two others knew where you were at all times. I told two people I was going to my new friend's home and pointed to the house. My young friend walked me to his grandfather's home directly across the street to introduce me to him and his sister. As we walked up to the entrance of his home, the grandfather stood in the doorway on two crutches, smiled, nodded his head, and said hello in Spanish. He welcomed me into his home without hesitance. My young friend was proud of his grandfather and wanted me to see his humble home. Neither one was embarrassed or ashamed to have me there.

The homes were clustered together in a small area, with either dirt or cement floors. The women spent all morning sweeping and washing. They took great pride in everything they had. There were no windows. In one cement room there were two beds high on cement bricks, two tall, old dressers, and a small television. What we would consider a kitchen was one large room without a stove, sink, or cabinets. Behind that room was a large room where there was another mattress on the floor along with other belongings. The home had a small cement area with a door where there was a toilet and a shower. Because of no sewers or anywhere for the water to flow, after using the toilet you would put the paper in

a bucket and it would be empted, I know not where. Grandfather was so caring. He told the entire team that whenever it was necessary, we were welcome to use the bathroom in his home. He was a special and loving man. After I left his house I cried for many different reasons. One big reason was that I wished I had been a little better prepared to speak in Spanish so I could communicate with them, and to thank them and tell them how much I appreciated and loved them.

*Rich and poor have this in common: The
Lord is the Maker of them all
(Proverbs 22:2).*

We drove to our hotel. Jerry and Randy signed us all in. We were given our keys and told to meet in one hour. We were about twenty to twenty five minutes away from the area we were having our tent project. Before we headed back we still needed to have our devotional time and eat dinner.

One of the best parts of this ministry was, while back in Georgia we paid a flat fee which covered all expenses on the trip. Whenever we went out to eat, our leader would pay the bill for us. We did not have to worry about how to pay in Mexican money which was a good thing, because a few of us had no idea how to do the money exchange.

The streets in Mexico were bumpy, with large potholes and speed bumps every so many feet so the cars were not able to speed. The potholes were hard on the tires and mufflers. I could see why they had to keep changing tires all the time.

Once the tent went up we were able to set up areas needed for the various ministries. There was an area for the doctor to see patients. A mobile pharmacy was set up using pieces of plywood as counters to hold the medicines, which were all stacked correctly for distribution. There were three team members helping with paperwork and the dispensing of the medicines. One of the women was to take blood pressures, and our translator was to help translate to the patients how to take the medicine and their proper dosages.

Another area was set up for our dentist. He had brought his portable dental chair, which was put up on cement bricks to raise the patient high enough for him to work comfortably. We were fortunate to have a dental technician with us to assist him. She was a joy to be with and a great help to the dentist. On his other trips he'd had to train someone on the spot, which could be difficult, time-wise. In one of the vans we had brought all his portable machines and tools for filling and pulling teeth. From the minute we arrived in the morning until the very last minute in the late afternoon the dentist and his assistant worked without any rest. Our dentist wanted to help every last person in this area, never turning any one away if he could help it. For most of the people in this area it was the first time they had been to a dentist. He was so gentle, but still there were cries from the young children and pain, of course, from the adults that had to have teeth pulled. I could certainly relate to their pain, because in my experience no matter how much you try to numb the mouth there is still some pain. I can watch others have work completed in their mouths, but I am chicken little when it comes to sitting in the dentist's chair myself!

In front of the main large tent were the small hook-up trailers that stored all the food that was needed to feed the people who would be there for lunches each day. There were large metal pots that were used to heat food such as pasta, sauce, and hot dogs. The ministry served over 500 lunches in three days. I must say the food was the best I had eaten in a while. There were four team members helping with the food each day. Their work was preparing, cooking, washing, and cleaning up. There was extra food so the people were able to take some home to their family members who were not able to attend, and also for their dinner that evening. Our cooks did a fabulous job with all the meals that were needed.

Grandfather let us hook up to his electricity and water which was a blessing for us the entire time we were there. The ministry paid his bills for the time we used his utilities.

Finally we were set up and ready to go. It was an exciting time to see everything just falling into place so beautifully. I couldn't believe it – I was really in Mexico! ... and I was willing to do whatever it was that Yeshua wanted me to do.

I prayed, *Lord, please use me the way You want to use me. If there is anything in my soul that is not right with You, please take it away. I want to be the clay, and please mold me into the person You want me to be. I am here to serve, not to be served, and I want to have nothing stand in the way. I thank You, Lord, that you allowed me to be here to do Your work. Put me in the places You want me to be and remove me from anything that I do not need to be a part of. Put Your angels around all of us and keep us protected.*

Thank you, in the precious name of Yeshua.

Chapter 15

Be Careful What You Pray For

On the way back to the hotel from the tent project I prayed for God to change me, to empty me of my old self, and to make me a new creature. I knew that I could not help others if I wasn't praying regularly and was feeling that I could do it all by myself. Pride is not acceptable in any form of ministry. I first looked at the Hispanic people and pitied them for not having much food, water, clothing and a decent home. I was wrong. They feel they are very rich in what they have. I wept for myself more than for them. I thought I had everything only to find out they have much more. At this point I realized it was I who needed to change.

The second night around ten o'clock, upon returning to the hotel after eating dinner I began experiencing stomach cramps; this escalated to feeling nauseous, and then I started vomiting. Virginia and I thought maybe it could be food poisoning. I got into bed and Virginia prayed for my peace, protection, and for relief from the ailments that I was experiencing. I told her maybe I should just stay in tomorrow. We both knew that God would not bring me this far to let me be sick and not able to serve. As I lay in bed I was having cold chills and couldn't seem to get warm enough. Virginia put a blanket over me, and that was when she began to sense an uneasiness in the room.

All of a sudden, God opened her spiritual eyes, and above my bed she saw a vision of a spiritual battle going on between good and evil. We turned out the lights. Virginia shook her head, turned her back on the scene, and tried to put it out of her mind. When she looked again, the vision was still there. She said she could only describe it as many white angels, approximately a foot in height, tumbling around in the air, battling with a dark gray, black mass as it tried to swoop down onto my body. As the dark mass came close to my head, the white angels would push it away from me, and they would battle again. As she described it to me, just as the black cloud was moving near my head, I woke up and jumped out of bed with stomach pains and ran to the bathroom. At that point the scene disappeared. We put the lights on. Virginia looked at me and knew we were in a spiritual battle, but not knowing exactly what was going on, she was very much aware that this was more than she wanted to handle by herself. It was time to call her husband Jerry and his roommate to pray with us. Their room was only three doors away from us. They quickly dressed and ran to our room.

Jerry and Virginia have been married for years and have worked together very closely in the areas of prayer, deliverance, and healings. I felt completely safe with them. They walk close with Jesus and listen to His every word and direction.

As Jerry and his roommate entered the room, Virginia told them what had happened and that she felt I needed intense prayer. Something was trying to attach itself to me. I was in another world. Not only was I sick with cramps but I couldn't and didn't know how to pray for myself. Virginia, Jerry, and his roommate began praying for me. They had been praying for about an hour when there was a knock at the door. Virginia asked who was at the door and they said it was our cook and our dentist. They had just flown into Monterrey that evening and had arrived late due to a two-hour delay leaving Atlanta.

They had taken a taxi from the airport, grabbed a quick sandwich, and were going to their room when they saw the light on in our room. Virginia told them to come in and start praying, even though they did not know the full extent of why they were praying. They soon found out! A spiritual battle was taking place in our room, and I believe God sent them to our room to fight for me.

I could hear Jerry and Virginia praying aloud, but something in me didn't want them touching me or praying for me. I couldn't stand to hear Virginia's voice as she prayed for me. I began coughing like I needed to vomit. One of the men placed a garbage can between Virginia and me. I remembered thinking that every time I heard Virginia pray I wanted to punch her in the face. I believe God was there in a small place in my mind telling me that she was my friend and that I should not harm her. The more she prayed and the louder her voice became, the more I hated that sound.

Virginia asked me if I had cleansed myself of all the things in my life that were keeping me from a close personal relationship with God. I felt a hand pushing on my back to help me say the words. I heard myself releasing pride, stubbornness, rejection, hatred, unfaithfulness, trust, anger, fear, deceit, my past sinful lifestyle, and possible other things that I do not remember. As I named each of these things, Jerry would command them to come out in the name of Jesus. As they were called out, I would cough and vomit into the garbage can.

After another hour of praying, Virginia sensed that the Holy Spirit was telling her to have those in the room pour anointing oil on their hands and lay hands on me as they prayed. At this point, Jerry poured a half a bottle of anointing oil on my head. Within thirty seconds I was tearing at my hair, scratching, trying to get it off of me. I became very agitated at the thought of losing the battle that was raging within me.

After confessing those things that needed to be released, there was an indescribable peace that came over my entire body. With my eyes still closed, I saw a vision of seven white objects flowing in a circle. In the middle of the circle was something large, round, and black. All of a sudden, one of the white objects used a very large sword to penetrate completely through the black circle. The black circle then disappeared. The seven white flowing objects then went above each one of us in the room, touched our heads, and also disappeared. I felt as though I was a new creature, molded to be what Yeshua wanted for me. I felt different ... so cleansed. Somebody asked if I was alright. They knew by the look on my face and the calmness in my body that I was fine.

Those in the room decided they would not mention to the other team members what had happened that night. Several of them were attending their first mission trip and it was felt that some may not understand what I had just gone through. I had gone through a deep deliverance of things not sanctioned by God, so that I would be able to walk down a righteous path with our Lord and Savior. We serve such an awesome God!

The others left to get some much-needed sleep while Virginia and I talked for a short time. I was told that by the time Virginia and I were ready to settle down it was three in the morning and we had to get up by six o'clock a.m. No problem! God was in control and we knew He would take care of us.

On a lighter note, our cook and the dentist relayed the following story: As they were approaching their room, which was one or two doors from Jerry and his roommate's room, they noticed the door to their room was standing open. They went to investigate, saw the door open, looked in and noticed the bed covers thrown back, Jerry's glasses on the table, both men's shoes on the floor, and their watches on the nightstand. They informed us later that they thought the rapture had occurred and they had missed it!

When I awakened three hours later, my body was not tired. I was ready for the day. I felt different, acted different, and others definitely knew I was calmer and more relaxed. They didn't ask questions, but several stated they sensed a change in me and were excited to see God working in the team.

My prayers for others became softer and yet spoken with more authority. The next day I felt led to sit on the ground praying for people, specifically by holding, praying for, and touching their feet. I wanted to pray for the feet that walked on the grounds the Lord had made. I prayed for protection wherever they went, and that the Lord's presence would be felt from the top of their heads to the bottoms of their feet. I felt that I was now able to serve others. The peace in my heart was so life-changing. I will remember the time and place God came and molded me into His creation. Whenever I begin to get nervous, scared, or agitated, I ask the Lord to please place me back into that peace I felt on the night He changed my life.

During worship the last evening in the large tent, I sat in the back next to one of the team members, and on his right sat his wife. We were standing and praising the Lord as the music played when suddenly I started weeping. As he looked at me, he said nothing, but put his arms around me and held me tight. He later told me that he felt he was not to speak, but to just hold me.

All of a sudden, as I closed my eyes, I saw two hands holding my heart, prying it open to let everything out that needed to be released. It was a completed work; nothing else was left that needed to be removed. I was truly cleansed from the inside to the outside, and it was over. I had received all that I prayed for and I was going home as a completely new creature. I was so thankful for my friend's silence, for not asking questions, and for his total support in a moment when I needed it the most.

I am thankful for our entire team. Each one of us had something special to offer at the correct time it was needed. Isn't it great how God is a God of second, third, even fourth chances? All we need is to be willing. When I first said yes to joining the mission tent project, I thought I could pray, I would help feed and maybe have a positive impact on the Mexican people. By the time I was ready to leave, it was the other way around. The people around me all week prayed for me, they fed me, they loved on me, they cared for me, and they showed how the love of God still works within them despite their financial hardship.

Their smiles, laughter, and constant desire to help has changed my heart inside and out. I never thought, or even imagined, that my mission trip would have turned out the way it did. I am so thankful each and every day for the mercy God placed in my heart. I return to that time of peace many times a day for a refreshing of my Lord's love. I remind myself daily of what He has done in my life, and I ask how I can show and give this peace to others. Thank you, Yeshua, for changing me inside and out.

My plans are to return to Mexico to see these people one more time. I keep wondering what He will have in store for me next time. I can hardly stand the wait. Whatever it is, I am more than willing to receive it. It is so simple ... just say "yes, Lord."

Chapter 16

Witnessing God's Healing Powers

Outside the main tent and a little off to the side, a smaller tent was put up. This tent was used for our prayer team. There were three of us from our team who stayed in the tent the entire time. All the rest of our team were welcomed to come in and out as they felt led to pray. From the home team in Mexico there were eight members. Pastor Gonzalo was able to come the first day and spend some time with us, and his wife, Grace, came and spent the second day with us. They were an inspiration to all of us. It was a blessing to see the genuine love they have for their people.

When the prayer tent was first put up, one of the team members suggested we build an altar of twelve stones as a remembrance to the Lord, just like the Israelites did in the Old Testament when they crossed the Red Sea. We collected the rocks and then we stacked them to the left side of the entrance to the tent. On the ground, in the center of another area off to the side, a cross was made out of rocks. A large cross, which had been anointed with oil, was put on the other side. On the ground in the middle of the tent there was an area where there were a few rocks that looked like a mountain and every time someone stood on top of these rocks, something beautiful and special seemed to happened.

The morning Grace was with us was unbelievable. During the first three hours she was able to lead eleven people to salvation through Jesus. They would come into the prayer tent, and before she prayed with them she would ask them if they knew Jesus. When their heads went side to side shaking 'no', she knew it was her time to tell them about salvation: how their sins could be forgiven and how Jesus could make a difference in their lives. She would ask if they understood the love He has for all of us, and then she would ask if they wanted to dedicate or rededicate their lives to Him. Some would cry and nod their heads yes, and then Grace would lead them in the sinner's prayer. If children were there with an adult, Grace would ever so sweetly bend down and explain to the child what their parent or friend had just talked about and the reason why. She would then tell them the same story about Jesus and would ask if they also would like to receive Jesus into their heart. Most of them said yes. Grace never went into long and drawn out stories; her explanation of salvation was plain, simple, and to the point. It has now made a difference to me how I share with others. From the first day to the last there were a total of eighty salvations.

From the very start I fell in love with the country and the people. I was blessed to be in the prayer tent the entire time, and to be able to see God's work up close was incredible.

Grandfather, the older gentleman who let us use his home and the family member of my little friend, came into our tent with crutches under both arms. He told us he'd had an accident many years ago, and ever since he'd had difficulty bending his leg. He could not walk without crutches. The team prayed for him in English and Spanish. I remember thinking it sounded like angels were singing with us. He thanked us, and when he started to leave I asked through an interpreter how he felt. He answered in Spanish that he felt alright. I looked at his face, which seemed different. I tapped him on his shoulder and touched his crutch showing him that he should put it down and try to walk without it. He took one crutch away and gingerly bent his knee to test it; when he realized he could bend it without difficulty, a huge smile spread across his face and he started walking around the tent. He then knelt down next to the chair, put his head on it, and started to cry. He was healed, he said, and he could walk without pain. His granddaughter was standing next to him, so he gave her the crutch, stood up, and they started walking out of the tent to his home across the street. The team began clapping and praising the Lord, giving honor to Yeshua. Everyone in the main tent started clapping also, even though they didn't know what had happened. When we told everyone Grandfather was healed, they all cheered with excitement. I believe he was healed because he gave of himself to others. He let us all use his home for the bathroom, water and electricity any time of day or night, without question. I felt God healed him to honor him. Every time we needed to use his home he would stand in the doorway with open arms and a big smile on his face that went from ear to ear.

A man and his wife came into the tent wanting prayer for his right ear. He had never been able to hear out of it. We prayed for the ear to drain of whatever may be trapped in there. Suddenly liquid started pouring out of his ear. It was not wax, nor pus from an infection, but rather it was just a thick liquid that ran out of his ear quickly, and suddenly he could hear. His face looked as though he was in shock. He couldn't believe God had healed him. He could now hear all of us speaking in a low tone. Once again, praises and clapping were offered to our Lord Yeshua.

A young child had come to the tent with a very high fever, too ill to walk, play, or eat. After praying for him, his fever went away that evening. He was also sent to the doctor to have him checked out and he was given some medicine to take home.

A five year old boy came into our tent screaming with pain in his left leg. The story his mother told us was the little boy was not feeling well so she took him to a witch doctor, whom she said was a

Christian. The witch doctor had prayed over him and put oil all over his leg. He was very sick and all the mother wanted was to get him help in whatever way she could. He came to us yelling, "The pain the pain!" He was bent over and could not straighten up. I had not idea what was going on. I wasn't listening to the story, but I did feel led to just start praying. The team stood behind and around him praying, while I sat down on the dusty ground. Sitting next to me was one of the other prayer team members listening to the story and praying in Spanish. I wrapped my hands around this child's thigh and started praying. As the pain started moving down the child's leg, the prayer team prayed louder and more intensely. They felt the power of the Lord working in this child. The young child was yelling to the man next to me, "Go lower, the pain is going lower." We then laid hands on his knee and prayed. The child cried, "Go down!"

We prayed while touching his calf, and suddenly the pain was completely gone. He stood up, wiped his tears, said all the pain was gone, and then ran out of the tent jumping up and down. He was pain free and now able to play with the other children. He continued to play the entire time we were there. I remained sitting on the ground completely drained, exhausted, and praising God for the miracle He had just laid upon this child. The team cried, clapped, hugged one another, and loved on his mother, who was so grateful. We were a true team, all working together for the good of God.

To be able to be a part of this miraculous time was more than I could've ever asked for. I cried like a child, hugged everyone, then just sat down on a nearby chair, overcome with amazement. God is so awesome; He loves His children more than we can imagine, and to watch one of them be healed was almost more than I could fathom.

A woman came in with sharp pains and a lump in her lower right pelvic area. She could feel it and said it had been there for a while. After the team finished praying for her, the pain was gone. She kept pushing into the area where the lump had been and couldn't feel it. We all cried and clapped our hands with joy. Another one for the Lord! All day I watched her pushing on her side as she checked to see if the lump had come back, but sure enough, it was truly gone. She was so excited. When I saw her in the evening service, she was completely free of pain.

One woman who looked to be in her late seventies asked for prayer. All she wanted was to come closer to Jesus, to be able to do what He wanted her to do, and to help others. But more than anything, her greatest desire was to know Him more.

If this is how it feels to be in heaven with the Lord, all sickness gone and with everyone filled with peace and joy, then I can't wait. Praying for the blessings everyone received the entire time we were in the prayer tent became draining by the end of the day. It was so much to take in at one time, it was almost unbelievable.

One day Jerry brought lunch to Virginia and myself in the tent, because we didn't want to miss one single thing. Another day Virginia and I were pulled out by Jerry to eat lunch in the lunch tent. We ate so fast, indigestion could have had a heyday inside us. We were covered in prayer and sent off and running again. Each day was more exciting than the last.

The days of our ministry were coming to a close and none of us wanted to return home. We all wanted to stay longer, but knowing we couldn't we promised everyone we would return.

Chapter 17

Don't Judge a Book By Its Cover

You can really get to know others well by spending ten hours traveling in a van together. Besides eating, snacking, and sleeping, there is plenty of time for a great deal of talking.

In the van I was riding in from Texas to Mexico, there a total of seven of us. Our team leader was the driver, and next to him was his co-pilot — a tall gentleman who was soft spoken and knowledgeable with maps. He hardly spoke during our drive. From the other team members I would hear laughter, jokes, and stories about their other missionary trips and their families. Still, he remained quite. I kept thinking, *What is wrong with him? Does he enjoy traveling? Does he like any of us? Will he keep quiet the next week?* Occasionally he would smile and read the directions to our driver.

Do not judge, or you too will be judges. For in the same way you judge others, you will be judged, and with the measure you use, it will be measured to you (Matthew 7:1).

Hallelujah, we finally arrived at the church in Mexico that was hosting us. We were greeted with hugs and kisses and escorted inside. I walked down towards the front and sat in a pew on the left side. As I looked around the sanctuary seeing where everyone was sitting, way in the back on the other side, I saw the man who had been our co-pilot. He sat close to a young girl who was holding her younger brother on her lap. Her brothers' legs were thin, but they were longer than her lap so I knew he had to be older than an infant or toddler, and I also noticed that his head hung over her shoulder. As I looked at the children, suddenly an arm came from behind them and rested on the young man's head. The co-pilot had put his hand on the boy's head and was quietly praying for him.

Large tears fell from my eyes. I was touched by the gentleness of this man. His heart was so sincere for those children. The little boy he was praying for has Cerebral Palsy. He is not able to sit up or feed himself, nor does he have any muscle control. This gentleman gave genuine love to both of them. Walking towards the back of the church, I went over to the co-pilot and gave him a hug.

As I stood and made my way to the bathroom, I knew in my spirit that I had been wrong about him. I had misjudged him. I had formed an opinion about him when I knew nothing about him. I had only looked on the outside of a person, not at his heart. I had judged him for all the wrong reasons. It was at that moment God taught me another lesson – that concerning the people I do not know, I am to stop putting them in a box and wrapping it tightly up.

When we were standing outside in front of the church, the co-pilot brought out from the van a large stack of papers. He had made copies of maps and information of our surrounding areas. He went through a lot of trouble to keep us informed. I admired him for that. He read to us some of the issues we could possibly get into, and asked if we had any questions. I was so impressed with him by this time that I wanted to learn more about his life.

The rest of the week we talked and started to get to know one another better. His job was to film the entire event. All the children stayed with him, laughing, jumping, and trying to help him as he videotaped. They enjoyed playing it back and watching themselves on camera. The co-pilot loved having the kids around him, and they truly loved him.

The Lord does not look at the things mans looks at. Man looks at the outward appearance, but the Lord looks at the heart (1 Samuel 16:7).

Directly across from the prayer tent was the dentist's chair. Many times I would look over and see the co-pilot praying for the children who were scared or crying as they waited to see the dentist or when they were having their teeth drilled for the first time. He held the hands of the men and women, closed his eyes, and prayed silent prays for them. He is a lover of all.

The co-pilot had also become very attached to my little friend, the one whose grandfather was so generous to our team. On the last evening of our project, pictures were taken and many tears were shed. As we were saying our last good-byes, the co-pilot took off his hat he had been wearing all week and gave it to our little friend. When I saw the tears in his eyes and our little friend crying, it touched my heart so deeply I had to walk away. We returned to the vans, not a dry eye among us. We waved and blew kisses to our little friends, and then we drove away. They tried to catch up with us, crying. I felt such a deep heartache over leaving them, but all I could think as I looked out the window was, *I will return, dear friends, I will return.*

I have kept in contact with the co-pilot. He is a dear friend and will be returning with the team when we go again in September. Watch out, Mexico, here I come!

Chapter 18

I Can Breathe

It was the first night of a two and a half day conference in Newnan, Georgia. Four of us had driven down together in one car. Normally it would be a forty-five minute drive, but due to traffic it ended up taking almost an hour and a half to get there. We were to meet seven other friends that evening at the hotel. As we were signing in at the registration desk the rest of our group showed up. We all went to our room to unpack our suitcases and freshen up. In twenty minutes we would meet in the lobby. Before going into the conference hall we decided we would go out to dinner.

By the time we were escorted into the conference hall, the downstairs seats were all filled. The only place left to sit was up in the balcony. There must have been at least four to five hundred people gathered in the hall, which was a breathtaking sight. It was exciting to see so many people at one time at this conference. Before tonight I had not heard or attended a conference with the three men speakers we were about to hear over the next three days.

Downstairs on the main level off to the sides were women waving many beautiful, colored banners during the worship of music. On the far left side of the stage, a woman was painting in colored paints whatever she felt the Lord was leading her to paint. When she finished we would have a chance to interpret what we felt was depicted in her painting.

The music was fulfilling to my mind and relaxing to my soul. We raised holy hands, jumped to the beat, and waved our hands high above our heads. The glorious sound of many voices singing in one accord could have moved mountains.

While sitting in the balcony, I suddenly felt a rushing in my heart and chest. I started drawing deep breaths and letting them out with full force. I remember thinking to myself, *why am I breathing like this?* This continued for about ten minutes. This deep breathing felt good. I did not feel nervous like I normally do when I'm having a problem with allergies, or when my lungs are not getting enough air. I didn't understand what was happening, but it felt good and I was excited.

One of the speakers explained how people had been healed through prayer. He had heard of others having been healed while on the phone. He shared with us how others with different types of diseases had been healed through the power of the Lord. He shared with us how some had even been raised from the dead, while others had been healed when all medical efforts had failed and the doctor had given up hope.

This was refreshing to hear and it gave me a new understanding about prayer. I had been taught that that healing could only take place by the laying on of hands, meaning touching the other person while praying for them. But even Yeshua did not always touch people to heal them; He would just speak to the person or the problem and tell them they were healed. He spoke with authority and passion. I believe this is what He wants us to do as well. It is not necessary to lay hands on others. Screaming, hollering, or trying to scare the other person to make them believe they have to quickly release their problem is definitely not God's way. Healing is not because of our ability; it is not by our might that we heal others. This is the Lord's work, and it is achieved whenever He is ready to heal someone.

Attending with one of the speakers was a team from a school of worship and supernatural ministry and prophecy from California. There were approximately fifteen to twenty men and women on this team. As they all stood across the stage facing the people in the auditorium, one at a time they were given the microphone to give words of knowledge they believed the Lord was giving them for others in the room.

The fifth person was a young gentleman who said there was a person who had once smoked for a long time but does not smoke now, but as a result they have emphysema. I nudged my girlfriend next to me on the left and asked her what he had just said.

I wanted to make sure I'd heard correctly. She said, "Emphysema." I yelled out, "That's me, that's me!" I claimed the healing. Again I started taking deep breaths, but this time I knew why I was breathing so deeply and heavily. The man asked if that word of knowledge pertained to anyone in the building. I raised my hand but he did not see me because of the lights. I knew it didn't matter whether or not he knew, because I knew and God knew. I had been healed and I claimed it. After the service I did not tell anyone except the people who were riding in the car with me.

Therefore I tell you, whatever you ask for in prayer, believe that you have received it, and it will be yours (Mark 11:24).

The hotel where all of us were staying was supposed to be a smoke-free hotel, but when we went into our rooms, we all noticed the foul smell of cigarette smoke. The hotel staff had tried to mask the smell with some air freshener spray and carpet cleaning, but it did not take away the smell. No one had a choice but to stay. There were no more rooms in the hotel due to the conference. Every other time I had spent an evening in a hotel and the smell of smoke was all over the beds, curtains, and carpet, I would have serious breathing problems. I would sneeze, get red itchy eyes, and my lungs would be tight. I would cough, wheeze, and continually gasp for air, needing to take inhalers.

When it was time to retire for the night, I put on my pajamas, got into the bed, prayed, took a deep breath, and went to sleep. It was amazing that I had no coughing spells or difficulty breathing, I knew God had healed me. There would have been no way I could spend the next two nights in that room and not end up in the emergency room with filled-up lungs and difficulty breathing if God had not healed me. I kept waking up all evening, taking deep breaths, letting them out, and thanking God for my healing. When I got up the next morning I felt wonderful and healthy.

I took my shower and prayed for a long time, thanking God for what He had done for me. I then dressed and went downstairs to join the others for breakfast. Still at this time I did not mention my healing. I was concerned all night for my dear close friend, because she also has difficulty breathing and coughing whenever she's around cigarette smoke. When I saw her the next morning, unfortunately she was coughing, which lasted that entire day and continued for the next two days. Thankfully, during the remainder of the conference I was as healthy as could be. I had no difficulty with smells, smoke, sleeping, or eating.

As the day went on I told the others what had happened to me the first night. They were encouraged and excited for me. I was a testimony for all of us that God is in the business of providing healing for His children.

We were all so excited to get back to the conference for the second session that we left the others eating at the hotel and told them we would save them seats. There were so many attending, and we wanted to sit on the ground floor this time. That meant we needed to go stand in line early. When the doors opened we were able to walk in and get great seats all together downstairs.

Once again the music was earth-shattering. There were many more young adults that day than the night before. They jumped, shouted, and sang as loud as they could to the music. It was exciting to see how they loved Yeshua and how they weren't embarrassed to sing to Him. When one of the speakers came up to speak again, everyone sat with ears opened. Afterwards he had a time for book signing for those who had purchased any of the books he had written. I, of course, just knew I had to buy one of his books, and when I reached the table where he was signing the books, I told him of the experience I'd had the night before. He did not even look at me. He signed his name and said it was nice to meet me. I thought he had not heard me or just wasn't interested. When we went into the conference hall for the next session, right before he started to pray, he explained again about healing. He asked where the woman was that he was just talking with who had been healed the night before. I raised my hand, and he asked me to please stand up. I stood up, clapped, turned around to the left and right, then to the people in the back, and then I jumped for joy, thanking and praising the Lord. The rest of the people clapped also. The speaker said, "Isn't it great to be happy and so excited for the Lord." During the rest of the conference people congratulated me on my healing. They were excited to hear my story.

Ever since that conference I have been walking around continually taking deep breaths. It feels so good to be able to breathe so deeply. I am so thankful that God watches over me all the time and gives me what I really do not deserve. I pray I can become everything God wants me to be to others. because He is loving, caring, protecting, and willing to help whenever anyone needs it. I will try never to look the other way or hide when someone is in need of my help or my prayers. I will continue praying daily to become a better person, one of whom God will be proud..

Chapter 19

God Still Moves Mountains

As I write this it has been six scorching hot months in Georgia since my first trip to Mexico, and time seems to have gone by so slowly. There has been no rain, and the flowers, bushes, and grasses have been dying all around us. The electricity bills are high, in the triple numbers, and now there is a complete watering ban. Mexico is not much cooler at this time of year, but I am on my way there to participate in my second mission trip, and this time I'm going prepared with large amounts of Gatorade and water.

Many times I have thought of the sweet memories of our new friends in Mexico to whom we had to say goodbye. In my photo album there are over three hundred pictures of their beautiful faces and the precious children at play. Often I have wondered, *will they still be there, or for one reason or another would they have had to move? Will they remember me and some of the funny times we had trying to communicate with each other?* I smile as I remember how our arms were used more than our mouths as we tried to figure out what we were saying to each other. My Spanish and their English really needed a great deal of translation. During both trips, there has been an interpreter with us, but they are not always available at the very moment when you need them.

Since my last trip I wrote in my journal a few prayer requests to God of what I would love to see happen to me on this trip. The first and most important is to be closer and have a deeper and stronger walk with the Lord. I want to hear and be guided more by His Holy Spirit, and experience peace like I have never felt before. There will be no sickness from allergies, no breathing difficulties, and my bronchial tubes will be clear. When I am to speak, I will speak with His love and wisdom. I would love to have a clearer understanding of His Scriptures. I would like to have more patience with others and to be at the right place, at the right time, for the right reasons. Let there be no confusion, nor fear of others. Please, dear Lord, bring me to a newer and deeper level of prayer.

The theme of this mission project was: God Still Moves Mountains.

The scripture was: *Everything is possible to the one who believes (Mark 9:23).*

This mission project consisted of seventeen members, eight women and nine men. Once again,

Randy was our team leader, Jerry was the head cook, and Virginia was in charge of the prayer tent. Pilot joined with us and one other woman who was with us last time. For a few members of our team this was their first mission trip, and I prayed it would change their lives and hearts toward others whose culture is different from ours.

Traveling on the road from Houston to Laredo, Texas, the skies in front of us were breathtaking. I was sitting in front on the passenger's side so I was able to get a clear view. Straight ahead were large, white clouds with a large, bright light in the shape of a round ball shining down in between them. In between the clouds was a large patch of bright blue. Below all the clouds were pink veils and a golden fire of brightness. The road ahead of us was lit up, guiding us on the path we needed to be traveling.

All around us on both sides were dark, black skies. Rain was in the distance all around us. As we continued to drive straight ahead into the light, the van passengers felt the peacefulness of the sky, and we tried to imagine how Moses must've felt when he was being led out of Egypt with God's protection surrounding him.

By day the Lord went ahead of them in a pillar of cloud to guide them on their way and by night in a pillar of fire to give them light, so that they could travel by day or night. Neither the pillar of cloud by day nor

> *the pillar of fire by night left its place in*
> *front of the people*
> *(Exodus 13:21-22).*

When we arrived at the church in Pan de Vida, the congregation was in the middle of their services. We walked in and sat in the back rows of the church so as not to disturb any of them. Pastor Gonzalo, his wife Grace, and their music team were singing and raising hands upward towards God, thanking and praising Him for today. We heard beautiful, joyful singing from everyone around us. Gonzalo had a smile of acknowledgement that lit up his face, and he was so glad to see we made it to the church in great timing. Looking around I was able to see many familiar faces. My heart felt as if it was skipping beats, and I wanted to rush over to kiss and hug them. When the service was over, I was able to go to the women and children to hug and love on them, and they saw tears of joy fill our eyes. I was truly home again. Not only did they remember me, they knew my name.

The people of Pan de Vida could not do enough to make us feel at home. They laughed with us, cried with many, loved all unconditionally, and made everyone feel, from the very beginning, like their own family. We were fed well, with all of them serving us. They worked with us side by side, making us feel welcome. They are truly loving friends, and that makes it hard to say goodbye. They touch the hearts of everyone who goes to work with them. It is a blessing to be able to feed them, clothe them, and sing, dance, and share our hearts with them.

Next to the church building was a plot of land that they could really use. The government told Pastor Gonzalo they would give the land to him. He began to get excited, only there was one stipulation: he would not be allowed to say or preach the name Jesus. Pastor thanked them, but declined. We are all praying for a change of heart within the government officials.

Adjacent to the small grassy land that's next to the church is an area where the government is building a multipurpose field for the children to play on. With all the children coming to the field, they will see the church and be invited in if they want to come. The church children will be able to use this multipurpose field also, so it's a blessing for all.

A large tent was set up for the main area where we had doctors, a pharmacy, and registration. On the outside to the left was a tent where the food was cooked for lunchtime. On the right side of the large main tent a prayer tent was set up. At the end of our afternoon each day the two smaller tents were taken down and then put back up again every morning. Jerry had his team cook for three hundred and fifty to four hundred every day. The meals were tasty and a treat for all.

In the prayer tent there were three of our team members and three of Pan de Vida's church members. They were strong and mighty in their prayers, and it was a blessing to be with them. It was interesting to see what they would do whenever there was a need for salvation; they had been taught which scriptures in the Bible pertained to the reason for salvation and how to receive it. The scriptures were highlighted, and as they read them to the requesting person, they both read together. The person was asked if they understood and if this was what they were wanting. When they agreed, a simple but beautiful prayer was said and a booklet was given to them to explain all that had happened.

Their address was written on a pad and given to the pastor, and at the end of the project he and his congregation would check up on each individual. The prayer team would then pray for whatever the person had on his or her heart that needed prayer. Some of the women came for prayer to receive more of the Holy Spirit in their lives. It was a time of a renewal of hearts.

This mission trip was so different from the last one in March. The mission work was the same as far as the purpose, but the area was different and the people who attended were from a different neighborhood. Some of the other children came, but not many adults. I felt this time for me was a teaching time. It felt as if I was in school each day with the Lord.

Each day I was in the prayer tent, I felt in my spirit that the Lord was teaching me many lessons about prayer. One important lesson I shared with my other two prayer partners was how our facial expressions can either help win hearts or turn people away. Let me explain what I mean. A man and a woman came into the tent. They sat down on chairs facing us. The woman had rough, broken skin with angry looking sores on her fingers, wrists, and feet. The other two women on our team made an involuntary face that said, *look, oh my goodness, how horrible,* and their eyebrows came down. The man saw their look and hung his head low. He looked embarrassed and ashamed. I felt led to pray for his wife's hands so I took paper towels, put them on her hands, and prayed. Virginia then prayed the same way for the woman's feet. The man then smiled at the woman, got up, and went out of the tent. Later that morning when they were leaving, the man came back to us and thanked us for praying for them. We smiled and nodded our heads, thankful that the Lord had been present with us.

Early one morning while we were getting ready to pray, the peace of the Lord came into my heart and spread all throughout my body. This was a very different, peaceful feeling than anything I had ever experienced before. The Lord laid it on my heart not to speak while others were praying but instead to just put my hands on their shoulders and pray for their peace. The Lord would take care of whatever they needed. After praying with a few women, I was led in the direction of our four team members who were cooking; I felt the Lord wanted me to pray for each one of them individually for peace and to have a blessed day.

Peace I leave with you; my peace I give you (John 14:28).

The Lord also showed me that, when praying for children, I was to be more aware of what they are doing. I was shown that I need to keep my eyes open and watch for crying, waving of the hands, and wanting to jump out of the person's lap they are sitting on, or if they are afraid of what is happening.

The weather was hot with an occasional light breeze. In the prayer tent we never heard the loud sounds of the large machines digging and plowing the field near us. At one point there were flying ants and mosquitoes in our hair and all over our clothes. After the field was watered down the bugs disappeared. We continued to pray and kept our minds solely on Yeshua. We had a job to do, and no bugs were going to interfere.

On our last mission trip we had met a four-year-old boy who suffers from Cerebral Palsy. He has a mother, brother, and sister who love him with all their hearts. They carry him, sing to him, and play with him, and they are always kissing his face. Last time his mother had to carry him with a waist band to hold him up. The boy is thin and frail, but is dead weight when being carried. This little guy has never spoken or walked. He is now getting some therapy and his mother works with his legs continually.

When she brought him in the first time, her desire was only that he would be able to walk. If he could only walk things would be a lot easier for her. He is still in a carriage and can only drink through a bottle. As long as his mother is within touching range, he smiles and even tries to laugh. He is very aware of when he is being held by someone else, and he cries. The minute his mother touches him he smiles and all the tears are gone. It is amazing how he can tell the difference between his mother's touch and that of another. We have all fallen in love with him and pray that his mother's wish is answered soon. He has touched the hearts of all those with whom he comes in contact. His mother is a patient, beautiful woman, and she has more patience for her son than anyone I have ever seen. *I pray, Lord, please help her and her family.*

We met two sisters ages seventy-seven and ninety-eight who live together in a small house. The younger one had just had head surgery, and she was also having chest discomfort. As the team prayed for her, the power of the Holy Spirit came into her and the peace she experienced left her sitting on the chair basking in His glory for several minutes. Her sister became concerned because she was not moving. She looked at her from the side, then put her hand on her back; I think she was trying to see if her sister was alright and still breathing. When the younger sister got up, she had so much peace on her face. She had a bright smile and said the pain in her chest was gone. They were two of the cutest older women I've ever known, and I pray they will live the rest of their lives together in peace and good health.

One young man came in for prayer because he was having trouble with his father and he wanted things to be better between them. As we all prayed, tears filled his eyes and the peace of God came upon him. He came back that evening to the service and was dancing with joy.

A woman who was working in registration was bitten by a bug and was given penicillin. After taking the first pill she had a strong reaction in the form of a rash with large bumps, and then a sore throat started. She came back that evening for prayer. After prayer, all her symptoms and rashes were gone. Praise the Lord once again; He is mighty!

I learned from the last trip that I needed to drink more liquids while enduring the hot, dry desert climate of Mexico. On the first day Virginia and I each drank two bottles of Gatorade and a few bottles of water. By the end of that day our ankles had swelled up to twice their size. The next day we mixed one bottle with half Gatorade, half water. Our ankles continued to swell up. The third day we decided not to drink any Gatorade, just water, but still there was no difference. Between standing on our feet all day, too much salt in the food, and just plain getting older, we gave up. We tried to keep our feet up as much as possible, but the swelling did not go down until we returned home.

One of the women from Pan de Vida made the team a wonderful, tasty treat. It was a large green apple on a stick with thick, dark, melted chocolate around it. When you ate the apple all the chocolate ended up on your nose, around your mouth, all over your fingers, and stuck to your teeth. We enjoyed every bite of it. Attached to the paper that was wrapped around the apple was a scripture, typed and laminated to use later as a bookmark once it had been washed.

The Scripture read:

Therefore, my dear brothers, stand firm. Let nothing move you. Always give yourselves fully to the work of the Lord, because you know that your labor in the Lord is not in vain (1 Corinthians 15:58).

Pan de Vida, Apodaca, Mexico

Going home at the end of a mission trip has been difficult for me both times because in so many ways it feels like home to me. I know Pastor Gonzalo is taking good care of his flock and that Jesus is watching over them. They are taught to teach, preach, and bring many into His kingdom, always glorifying Yeshua. I pray it will not be too long before I will be able to return and join in with my family in Mexico.

I truly thank you, Lord, for allowing me to visit and work with your children in Mexico. They have brought me great joy, and I hope to be able to spread all the valuable lessons You have taught me to all with whom I come in contact. May I be able to hear You say,

"Well done, my good and faithful servant."

Chapter 20

Please, Just One More Time

This tent project was set up seven blocks from the one we'd held in March. I wanted so badly to be able to see my heart-adopted grandfather, his grandson and granddaughter. I had heard that after we left the last time, Grandfather had to go back to using his crutches again. We found out a few months later that he has bone cancer throughout his body. He went to the hospital to have some treatments and was given some medicine to help with pain. There was nothing else they could do for him, so he was sent home. I prayed a selfish prayer; I asked God to please let him live until I could see him at least one more time. His grandchildren went to live with their father two days after we left in March. I was told by Pastor Gonzalo, the day after we left, the children still looked for us to come back. They wondered if we would ever return or if we would forget them. During the day I asked Randy if we could please go to Grandfather's home to see him for at least ten minutes. He said he would try to arrange it the next day. I prayed, *Lord, please let me see him just one more time.*

While I was singing and dancing to the music in the evening service, I looked to my right, and there sat Grandfather in his wheelchair. I cried and ran over to him and almost fell on top of him as I swooped down to hug him. He started to cry, patted my cheeks, and hugged me with the little bit of strength he still had. We held each other for a few seconds. Grandmother was standing next to him and I couldn't wait to hug her, too. When she had heard we were coming, she wheeled him though the streets in the dark to bring him to the evening service. On his lap was a bag of drinks and some medicine. He was frail, and his voice was no louder than a soft whisper. I asked him about his grandchildren and he told me they would be at the tent project the next night. *Thank you, Lord, for answering my prayers.*

Jerry also had a special bond with him. During the evening I watched as these two grandfathers sat together with tears streaming down their faces. Jerry put his hand on top of Grandfather's hand and they sat in silence. They had a smile on their faces and love in their hearts for one another.

All evening Grandfather kept holding his stomach and rubbing his arm, and I could tell he was in deep pain. It was difficult for him to sit for such a long time. His leg was painful, and he was having great difficulty sitting still. However, the music touched

Grandfather's heart, and the sermon of salvation touched him even more.

We did not realize Grandfather did not have salvation. When the time came for an altar call, he stood up, said the prayer and accepted Jesus into his heart. He felt better and had a peaceful smile on his face. When the service was over, he and his wife had to go home soon thereafter. I cried, but I knew I was blessed to have seen him again for one more time.

The next evening Grandfather came in his wheelchair carrying his crutches. His hair was neatly combed, he had put on a different shirt, he had a smile on his face, and no medicine bag on his lap. Grandmother told us that until last night he had not been able to bend his left leg because it had been so painful and very difficult to move. He had a rod in his leg from his hip to his knee. On this night he was able to bend his knee and stand on his leg. When it was time for testimonies to be given during the evening service, Grandfather stood up on his crutches and walked down to the front. In his little voice, he told how he had received Jesus the night before and now he could walk better and was not having as much pain. As he began crying, everyone cried also. He went back to his wheelchair and stood for awhile clapping and singing to the music. I believe it was all very overwhelming for him, and he later sat down in his wheelchair for support.

As I was helping and watching a young girl's dance ministry, I looked over at Grandfather, and there sitting with him was my little friend and his sister. I ran to them, hugged and kissed them and wouldn't let them go. My little friend of eleven is going to be a handsome guy. His hair was cut short and neat, and he was a little taller, but had a young man's face. His sister, who is ten years old, looks just like his twin. I felt selfish in one sense; I didn't want to share them with anyone. That was impossible, however, because everyone ran up to them and gave them hugs and kisses. The children's eyes became wet with tears. They were also overwhelmed.

In March my little friend had given me one of his bracelets so that I would remember him. I told him I would pray for him and his family every day and would return shortly to visit him. When we were ready to say our goodbyes, he put his arm around my waist and would not let me go. Here stood an eleven year old sobbing, no, no, don't go. It was more than I could handle at that time. That night I pointed to the bracelet and told him I had worn his bracelet every day, and that I had been praying for him and his family.

We were able to spend a few, short hours together and many pictures were taken. When asked if he would be able to return the next day he said they could not. It was time again to say our goodbyes. I first thanked his papa for bringing them that night. I kissed his sister and gave her a hug. There waiting for me stood my young friend looking at me with those sad eyes. Once again he held my waist and started to cry. I held him tight, kissed the top of his head, gave him a hug, and had to let go. Grandfather was waiting and standing with his crutches. He also cried when I hugged and kissed him, but he told me he and

Grandmother would be returning tomorrow evening, which would be our last evening.

We walked to our van, waved goodbye, blew kisses, and as we drove away they became only shadows in the distance. It had been a great evening. Their papa is doing a great job with them. They are in school and doing well. *Thank you, Jesus, for keeping them in your care.*

It was around ten-thirty the next morning when the children returned to the tent. Papa had seen how much all of us loved his children and how much they meant to us. He let them come back to visit with us for a few hours. It was another prayer answered. I had my obligations to the prayer tent during the week and I didn't want to let my prayer partners down. When we were able to take a break, I spent my time with the children. At some point when I was praying in the tent my little friends left. In a way, I was thankful I didn't have to go through the pain of saying goodbye and leaving them again. Last night would've been enough, and today was a bonus. I thanked God I was able to see them as much as I had. I was given their address so I could now write and keep in touch with them. I felt better this time and was relieved that they were fine. I will continue to pray for them every day and will try to see them as much as I possibly can. That night I would have one more evening with Grandfather and Grandmother.

They were there with the wheelchair because of the distance they had to walk. The crutches were alongside the chair, but when Grandfather stood up to clap to the music, he stood alone, with no crutches.

He even took a few steps by himself with no help. He was on a cloud, standing tall. The evening went great, and once again it was time for goodbyes. The entire team along with Grandfather and Grandmother had pictures taken together. Before we parted I told Grandfather I hoped to see him again. As he opened his arms wide he said, "I will be here waiting for you with open arms." I thanked God for our time together. At any time, if our good Lord chooses to take him before I can come back, I will remember his smile, his gentle bird voice, his open arms, and the love he gave to me.

Grandfather reminded me of my dad at the end of his life. He was smaller in statue than he had been in his younger years. They both walked in pain, but always had a smile. Their hands were frail, soft, and gentle to touch. Their eyes were the eyes of men who had experienced enough and wanted to go home. Even though we are from two different cultures, love speaks only one language – that of the heart. I had only known Grandfather a very short time, but he touched my heart forever. I will now be able to let go a little easier, once again. *Thank you, Lord, for our short but precious times together.*

I am thankful I had just one more time with my dad and with Grandfather.

Chapter 21

I Do

Since becoming a believer, my life changes have been miraculous. One important lesson I have learned on this journey is that life is not just about me. God created all of us very special in our own way, and He wants us to be the best we can be for His glory. I've also learned that being aware of other people's feelings, needs, and wants are essential to my living a healthy life.

In the beginning it was difficult for me to become a believer in someone or something I could not see or touch. Since believing in Yeshua, however, I have learned by faith that the Lord is always with me. As I read the Bible, which I believe is God's written Word, He guides me and leads me down the correct path.

Show me your ways, O Lord, teach me your paths: guide me in your truth and teach me,

*for you are God my Savior, and my hope is
in you all day long
(Psalm 25:4-5).*

I have hope where there was none before. God had given me a passion to know Him, to serve Him, to proclaim Him, and to glorify Him.

He is my bright morning star (Revelation 22:16).

I am moving forward to be what God has called me to be: his disciple and a follower of His words. It is important to me to make my life count. The Lord has walked with me through all of my dark and troubled times. I know He is always there for me to bring me into His light of hope. God has never found fault with me, and He always wants the best for me. Is it always easy? No, it is not, and therefore I am still in the learning process. Despite the ridicule of my family and some of my friends, I will press on, staying with the faith I have in Yeshua.

Now I proudly say with all my heart, "I'm a Jew, and yes, I Do do Jesus!"

A Time for Everything

*There is a time for everything, and a season
for every activity under heaven:*

a time to be born and a time to die,

a time to plant and a time to uproot,

a time to kill and a time to heal,

a time to tear down and a time to build up,

a time to weep and a time to laugh,

a time to scatter stones and a time to gather them,

a time to embrace and a time to refrain,

a time to search and a time to give up,

a time to keep and a time to throw away,

a time to tear and a time to mend,

a time to be silent and a time to speak,

a time to love and a time to hate,

a time for war and a time for peace.

Ecclesiastes 3:1-8

Glossary

Since I have become a Jewish believer, friends, and other acquaintances have asked me, "I work with other Jewish people in my office; how can I share the Bible with them?" Others wish to know what words they should use so as not to offend their Jewish friends while witnessing to them. Here are a few suggestions of words, phrases, and verses that have helped me in my walk with Yeshua and in sharing Him with others.

Instead of	*Use*
Jesus	Yeshua
Christ	Messiah or Mashiach
Christian	Believer, Follower of Messiah, Born-again Jew
Church	Congregation, Temple, Synagogue, Messianic Community
Baptize	Mikvah; (fully) immerse

Gospel	Good news (of the Messiah's atonement)
Pentateuch	Torah: First five books of the Bible
Old Testament	Old Covenant; Tenach
New Testament	New Covenant; B'rit Chadashah
Jehovah	The L-rd G-d of Israel, The Holy One, HaShema
Lord	Adonai; L-rd
Sin	Wrongdoing, breaking the commandments, lawlessness, sin
Devil	The adversary, Hasatan (Hebrew transliteration for satan)
Reverend, Priest	Pastor or Messianic Rabbi
Trumpet	Shofar
Communion	Remembrance of the Last Sedar of the Messiah
Wafer	Matzah, unleavened bread
Apostle	Emissary
John the Baptist	John (Yochannan) the Immerser (or Mikvah-man)
Glory of God	Sh-kinah
Hades/Hell	Sh'ol
Lamp	Menorah
Law	Torah

Passover	Pesach
Passover Meal	Sedar
Peace	Shalom
Sabbath	Sabbat
Siddar	Prayer book (contains prayers, scriptures, order of service)
The Shma	Jewish affirmation of faith, recited during all worship services. (Deuteronomy 6:4)

He would be a descendent of King David. (Jeremiah 23:5, 6)

The city of his birth would be Bethlehem. (Micah 5:1, 2)

He would have a divine nature. (Isaiah 9:5, 6)

He would be executed by crucifixion. (Psalm 22:14-17)

He would rise from the dead. (Isaiah 53:10)

Source used: The Jewish New Testament translation by David Stern, Messianic Judaism by David Chernoff

When orthodox Jewish people write the words God and Lord, they replace the o with a dash. Because of the holiness, deep respect, and reverence they have for our Lord, they will write the words "Lord God" as "L-rd G-d."

When a holy book, which is the prayer book or Bible, is dropped, the person who dropped it will kiss it after it has been picked up from the ground; this also shows reverence to our Lord.

Many Jews, and believers, follow the custom of touching and kissing a Mezuzah, which is a small box nailed on the doorpost of their home that contains scripture verses. They touch it with their fingertips, kiss them, and recite, "May God protect my going out and coming in, now and forever."

Printed in the United States
201214BV00001B/1-120/P